Every day before he went home Keeny Durán
stopped to look at the ugly flat roofs of the housing
project where he lived. He got a feeling of hopelessness. For him, the streets led to police stations,
reform schools, gangs, and drugs. But he didn't
have much to go home to—only a screaming mother
who trusted him as little as the rest of the world
did. Keeny gets into deep trouble one more time
and must decide whether to hide or come out in the
open and prove his innocence.

FRANK BONHAM has researched the Los Angeles
Watts area and his stories ring with the life, the
language, and the toughness of a city slum. He has
written many books for young readers, including
The Mystery of the Fat Cat, *The Nitty Gritty*, and
the widely acclaimed *Durango Street*.

Viva Chicano

Frank Bonham

Published by
DELL PUBLISHING CO., INC.
1 Dag Hammarskjold Plaza
New York, N. Y. 10017
Copyright © 1970 by Frank Bonham
All rights reserved
No part of this publication may be
reproduced or transmitted in any form
or by any means, electronic or
mechanical, including photocopy,
recording, or any information storage
and retrieval system now known or
to be invented, without permission in
writing from E. P. Dutton & Co., Inc.,
except by a reviewer who wishes to
quote brief passages in connection
with a review for inclusion in a
magazine, newspaper, or broadcast.
Reprinted by arrangement with
E. P. Dutton & Co., Inc.,
201 Park Avenue South,
New York, N.Y. 10003.

ISBN: 0-440-99400-4

RL: 5.9

Printed in the United States of America
First Laurel-Leaf printing—August 1971
Twelfth Laurel-Leaf printing—August 1982

Readers often ask the authors of books such as this one, "Is the story true? Did those things really happen? Did you know a Keeny Durán?"

Let me say at the outset, therefore: This story is true. There really was a Keeny Durán. The things that happened really did take place—not to one boy, however, and not in the order in which the events are here arranged.

The book is true, in the sense that nothing in it is false.

Joaquín "Keeny" Durán, the protagonist, is a blend of several boys I met in the course of gathering material for the story. You will find boys like him, his friends, and his enemies, in any big city—in police stations, jails, detention homes, housing projects, and on the sidewalks.

But although you may find them, they will not necessarily talk to you about their lives, loves, and problems—unless you can say, "So-and-so sent me."

The man who sent me is a gifted and respected parole officer named Kenneth R. Cilch, of the California Youth Authority. Mr. Cilch, to whom this book is dedicated, has dealt with hundreds of boys just out of Youth Authority institutions; yet to him each boy represents a worthwhile human being in need of help. Each boy is an individual; one of a kind; a potential winner. Boys try hard, sometimes, to prove to him that they aren't worth helping—too tough, too hyped-up, too black, too brown—but most of them finally admit to him that, Yes, they do need help; they are scared; they want to make it this time.

As a means of reaching the hard-to-help, Mr. Cilch often places a ward in a boardinghouse like the one in the book (known simply in San Diego as Parolee House). The boys make most of their own house rules and are responsible for their own behavior. This climate of responsibility seems to be what most of them need; the success rate of the boys at Parolee House is far greater than that of similar boys trying to make it in the dreary foster homes and Skid Row hotels where most of them live.

Mr. Cilch needs no thanks from me to feel appreciated: Seeing one of his boys get a job, finish school, or enroll in college is the kind of thanks he responds to. Yet I should be ungrateful indeed if I failed to acknowledge his help. He gave me invaluable aid in gathering material for, and in the writing of, this book.

Others who gave generously of their time and experience were Anita Spencer; Fred Closson, of the University of San Diego; Paul Parks, of Operation Hope, in Los Angeles; Arturo Serrano Holmes; and George Nishi-naka, of Special Service for Groups, in Los Angeles, through whose good offices I was able to reach many persons, and penetrate several well-defended agencies I should never have reached otherwise.

Chapter 1

A few blocks from the housing project, Keeny Durán stopped on a street corner to lean against a telephone pole and gaze down the hill into the flats below him. He dropped a loose-leaf notebook and some school-books on the curb at his feet. It was past four o'clock on a winter day. The sun had fallen behind the hill and the air had chilled, but the pole, still warm, exhaled a robust summer fragrance of creosote. Below him, the buildings of the Project were neatly fitted together in the forms of T's, E's, and H's, each building three stories high and flat-roofed. The boxy structures, dozens of them, were laid out like a puzzle to test the intelligence of rats. *Even a stupid rat,* Keeny thought gloomily, *would have sense enough to stay out of them.*

Every day he stopped here to lean against the telephone pole and gather strength to go home. But today a tide of hopelessness seemed to rise from the flats, engulfing him in an unbearable somberness.

Man, I can't hack it, he thought.

School was bad, but the apartment was worse. Everybody in the family yelled and nobody listened. It was a screaming madhouse, his mother screeching at the top of her voice, his new stepfather, who was out of work, and an *Anglo,* for Pete's sake, laying out poker hands in the kitchen, and grinning, always grinning.

Joaquín, I told you to do your homework! I'm going to call your parole officer, so help me—!

I already did it, Mom, Keeny would say.

I told you, Joaquín, if you don't keep your grades up, I'll turn you in myself. They'll send you back to Deuell. George, will you talk to this kid?

He said he did it, baby.

Estela, put down that eyebrow makeup!

Dimly Keeny remembered his mother when she was young and beautiful. But a screamer even then. She was still attractive, he supposed, with her dark eyes and glossy hair; at least she found husbands without any trouble.

From the Project, like a mist from its dead gray lawns, flat roofs, and leafless trees, the tide of hopelessness rose higher, threatening to drown him. He had an uneasy feeling that a half-healed wound in his mind was about to tear open. When it tore—as it had many times before in his seventeen years—he would suddenly become a different person, doing crazy things he would not normally do, the kind of things that had often landed him in Youth Authority custody.

Well, man let's go! he told himself. And he struck the heel of his hand against the telephone pole as though trying to split the wood. The pain in his fist made him catch his breath, but it cleared his head. He straightened and picked up his schoolbooks. Whistling, he crossed the street and headed down the steep hill. He wore a dark-blue tee shirt, black pants, and a white nylon barber's jacket; he had been learning barbering the last time he was in a Youth Authority institution, and they had let him keep the jacket. His face was calm, now. He had the thin, aristocratic features of a young grandee. His father used to tell him

8

that when he grew up he would look just like the Aztec kings on the calendars in the Mexican markets. But the kingly effect was partially spoiled by his hair. They had cut it short in prison, and it was at an awkward length now, thick and bristly.

Behind the easy front he wore, he began to feel still calmer. *I'll do my homework and split,* he decided. He had promised the Royal Aztecs he'd meet them in Old Town tonight, across the river, if he could get out. *I'll get out,* he told himself. The Aztecs were not exactly a gang, just a bunch of guys, though they liked to think of themselves as a gang. He smiled. Throw them up against some of the gangs he'd run with and they'd know for sure they weren't a gang.

The steep street was lined with tiny frame houses with small, gabled porches. Each little peak-roofed house looked as though a cuckoo might hop out of the door to tell you what time it was, like a wooden bird in a Swiss clock. Most of the houses were covered with fake brick siding in tan or green tones. In the yards were drifts of junk that told you what the houses really were: factories where children were produced, truckloads of them. The yards were an endless junk-heap of jungle gyms, dismantled toys, soggy dolls, broken bikes and trikes. On one roof there was an automobile tire.

There were shrubs and trees, but only the toughest of plants survived; castor bean and geranium grew as crazily as poison oak. The castor-bean shrubs were big, with shiny bronze leaves and spined seedpods that were poisonous. Everybody knew they were poisonous, but people planted them just the same, as though the army of kids that ran roughshod over the neighborhood needed some sort of pesticide to knock off a few of them now and then.

But it was curious how even in a place like this, a Mexican-American district known by the ridiculous name of Happy Valley, in a vast ghetto called Dogtown, people tried to carry on as though they *liked* it here—like there was a country club just around the corner. Keeny grinned at the dead palm tree some old guy had sawed off three feet high in his front yard; he had hollowed it out and planted geraniums in it! On the corner lived the Fern Lady, who had dozens of rusty buckets and tubs of ferns all over her porch and yard, big ugly sword ferns. Other people planted little orange trees and fenced them in with chicken wire to keep kids and dogs from demolishing them. But with all this yearning toward beauty, the plants were always stunted and dingy, infected with a black smut. It was as if the Big Gardener in the Sky were saying:

Whoops! Just a minute, folks. . . . A slum is supposed to be ugly. Here's a new disease for your rosebushes.

The Project began at the bottom of the hill; and that was where Uglyville *really* started. As Keeny neared home, the bad feeling returned. He felt as though he were sinking to the bottom level of a coal mine, where the air was so poisonous that you carried a canary with you: If the gas killed the canary, you were allowed to back out. He figured the canary would be sprawled on its back by now with its feet in the air.

The Project was like housing projects everywhere he'd ever been, something like an army camp. The buildings had been set down like shoeboxes; lawns lay flat and lifeless among them, tattered like hall rugs. Out in the dead grass, sycamore trees stood leafless and bone-white.. The three-story buildings were fingerpaint-colored—yellow, brown, green, and pink.

Keeny's, which he was now approaching, looked as though it had been painted with mud.

And just as he was walking toward the stairwell that rose like an open chimney through the building, splitting it into two equal parts, he heard his mother shriek, two stories up:

"Armando! My God, didn't you hear me tell you—!"

A hand grenade went off in Keeny's head. His cool blew to fragments. He did not stay to hear what she had told Armando, his baby brother. He turned and walked high-shouldered back toward the street that curved through the Project, muttering furiously to himself. He thought of the pills in his stash place in the flat. A few of them in him and she could scream her lungs out and he wouldn't care. But he'd been trying to go it without pills since he got out of Deuell six months ago. For pills and trouble were blood brothers.

In a daze, he crossed the street with its sparkling shrapnel of broken glass and wandered on through the Project, swinging a little key chain he carried with a big Mexican five-peso piece soldered to the end of it. He was not sure where he was going, but he was on his way. Strange things happened in Keeny Durán's head sometimes. He really had a spooky belief that his mind was occupied by another Joaquín who took over in crisis situations. Without having made any conscious decision to call his parole officer, he found himself standing outside the pay-telephone near the Project rental office, digging in his pocket for a dime. And after he found the dime, he thumbed a card out of his wallet and studied the fine print on it: FRANK BAKER, the card read. PAROLE AGENT. DIVISION OF PAROLE AND COMMUNITY SERVICES.

That's the idea, man, thought Keeny. *Little service, here, to a good customer. Earn your pay, man.*

When the parole officer came on the line, Keeny slumped into a cool, negligent posture and let his voice grow limp. "Hi, Mr. Baker? This is Keeny. Ha' you?"

The P.O. said bluntly: "I'm fine, Keeny. I thought we had a date last week."

"Yeah, I'm sorry about that. I had to baby-sit with my little brother."

"Why couldn't your sister do it?"

"She was supposed to, but she got home late."

"I see. Well, you know, I have only so many hours a day, Keeny, and I've got a hundred and thirty cases. When I make a date, I like a boy to keep it. Why didn't you call me?"

"We don't have a phone, Mr. Baker."

He did not know this new parole officer of his very well. Some P.O.'s were easy to con, some were as tough as a vice-squad cop. He came to attention in the booth, trying to plan ahead.

"Oh, no phone?" said the P.O. "What are you using now—a walkie-talkie?"

"A pay-phone. See, I didn't want to leave 'Mando alone and walk over here. It's a block away."

But then he began losing interest in the whole operation. He had called because this weirdo who lived in his skull, this other Keeny, had told him to. P.O.'s were supposed to help, and he had thought that maybe. . . . But, hell, how much help had any cop or P.O. ever been to him? *Help? Man, you've got to be kidding!*

Scratch one dime, he thought.

"Well, never mind," Mr. Baker said. "If I give you a new time now, will you keep it?"

"If I'm here."

"Oh, are you going to the winter Olympics or something?"

"Maybe. All I know is I can't hack it at home much longer."

"What's the problem?"

"My mother."

Mr. Baker's voice softened just a degree. "Oh? How's that?"

Keeny started explaining how it was. But as he talked, an angry feeling began to thrash in him like a speared snake. How *did* he really feel? he asked himself. *Trapped. Scared.* Scared of busting out again and getting locked up in another of the Youth Authority institutions that had been his home for at least a third of his life.

But up to now, all anyone had been able to tell him about his home life was that his mother had a hard time, that she needed him. Okay, but he didn't need her.

"You haven't met my new stepfather, have you?"

"No. Do you like him?"

"Man, I guess he's okay," Keeny said impatiently. "He's an *Anglo*," he added. "Right now he's in a thump over a bad check he gave. Every time I'm in the joint, she marries another freak!"

He heard her voice climbing hysterically, octave by octave, as she told her sad stories to the social workers who came to the flat.

My God, I didn't know what he was like till I married him! He was so nice to the kids. But after we were married he began getting these telephone calls from a girl—fifteen years old!

That was Enrique. Another, Florencio, was an arsonist who was always setting little fires. The new one, George, was a forger. Georger the Forger, Keeny called him, in telling the Aztecs about the antics of his new stepfather. Recently it had dawned on him that there must be something peculiar about a woman

13

who guessed wrong so often about men.

"Is he in jail?" asked Mr. Baker.

"He's out on bail," said Keeny.

"Well, I don't see how it involves you. You really haven't told me what the gut-problem is, have you?"

"I guess not. I don't know. Forget it. It's okay."

"No, wait a minute. Let's get this straight. Are you thinking of splitting?"

"No, I guess not."

"Because I'd have to revoke you if you did. And with your record, you might wind up with a Y-A number this time."

Keeny winced. One thing he did not need was a Y-A number. If you messed up in the joint with a Y-A number on your shirt, you could get busted over to an Adult Authority facility—a prison like San Quentin. Keeny swung the peso piece silently, looking at a series of locked doors in his mind.

Mr. Baker came on again, sounding friendly, now, sounding resolutely cheerful, like a green junior officer at Juvenile Hall. "I'll tell you what. Meet me at the taco stand across from school tomorrow. Four o'clock. Okay?"

"Okay. But if you're going to try to talk me into learning to love my lousy home, Mr. Baker, it's a waste of time. She never stops screaming, my mother. Man!"

"You'd like to be in a foster home, right?"

Keeny asked quickly: "Could I go back to Mrs. Dixon's?"

Mr. Baker chuckled. "I didn't know you'd been one of Rosie's boys. She got closed down."

"I know. But I thought she might be open again."

"Rosie's had it. That was a snake den, Keeny. Drugs, liquor, boys-and-girls-together. . . . Wow!" Mr. Baker laughed. "What I want to talk to you about is a sort of boardinghouse I'm interested in. I haven't brought it up before because I don't have the official blessing for it. I've got about a dozen parolees there. I'm not sure whether I could squeeze you in, because we're already over the number of boarders allowed, and I don't want the neighbors complaining. I'm not sure, either, whether the boys would like having another resident."

Keeny put in quickly, "If you said so, they'd have to like it, wouldn't they?"

"Not really. This place is more or less run by the guys, with the landlady having the last word on some things. We'll talk about it tomorrow. Since you're still a ward of the court, your mother couldn't put a stop to your going there. . . . You're not dropping pills, are you?"

"No, sir! I'm righteously clean, Mr. Baker," said Keeny, nobly. It was practically true. He was neither selling nor using drugs. All he owned was a small personal supply of stumblers, for emergencies.

Chapter 2

Keeny remembered the strong, loving man who had been his father—big, brown-skinned, and proud. Though he was only a laborer, he made fairly good money and did not leave it in the bars like so many other men who came home in hard hats. He had given Keeny and his sister three things: love, material things, and pride. Pride in *la raza,* the Mexican heritage. He made Keeny proud of looking like an Aztec prince. He told Keeny he would become a lawyer or a doctor; he would work to help *la raza.* He made him fight his own fights. And then one day, after a heavy rain, a ditch caved in on him, and he died. Keeny was six.

Keeny's mother, needing a man's strength, grew hysterical and *loca* and married a weak man she did not love.

The kids bothered the new stepfather. Keeny started school, where he learned that nothing much was expected of him but to be there. "Aim high, Joaquín," his teachers seemed to say, "be a laborer."

One day the stepfather burned Keeny with a cigarette to teach him to be quiet. Keeny ran away. The police found him hiding in an empty store two days later and booked him as a runaway. After a full day he told them his name. He was seven now and had a record.

After that it was stealing, truancy, and fighting; Juvenile Hall, boys' homes, Youth Authority institutions. Drugs, gang-fighting, and burglary.

But he never forgot his father, nor the gift he had given him: the pride, fine and shining, like a magic sword. But, unfortunately, it was the day of the gun, and this sword, which could get him into trouble, could not get him out. He did not particularly want it, but it was part of him. He was a *chicano*, and that was how it was.

That was how it was with him, and it might have gone on like that forever but for the wife of a supervisor the last time he was in the joint.

"You've got a good head, Keeny," she told him. "When are you going to start using it?"

Before he knew it, she had inveigled him into the prison library, and through the books he read, some things began to come into focus for him. A lot of fears surfaced; but a tender shoot called Hope sprang up. Turning seventeen behind bars settled things for him: He made up his mind to get out and stay out.

He had been out six months, now, and the shiny paint was wearing off his determination. It had become scratched and dulled in the madhouse called the flat. He was still hanging on, but beginning to doubt himself.

For two hours, tonight, a fire-fight raged back and forth through the flat. Keeny's mother was wild. Estela had been seen walking home with a boy. *Ay de mí!* At thirteen!

Little Armando had a runny nose; he must be catching that terrible disease the boy next door had come down with last week. The boy was still in County Hospital. And now George, Keeny's new stepfather, had admitted that the lawyer friend they were going to see tonight was not actually a lawyer. He had merely read some law once while he was in prison. But he knew all the angles, George insisted.

"Angles! Angles!" wailed Keeny's mother. "Angles enough and you go to the gas chamber! Joaquín, did you tell those Royal Aztecs what I told you?"

"Yeah, Mom. You couldn't drag them here."

"Royal Aztecs! Royal *Addicts!*"

She went to the door to check her locks. She had six of them—latches, chains, bolts. She was afraid a Mad Killer would break in and sink an ax in everybody's head. She went back to the kitchen, but a moment later Keeny heard her shriek and bang a pan against the stove.

"Estela! Put down that eye makeup and help Carlos! My God, eye makeup at thirteen! Wipe it off or I'll scrub it off with a brush! I *told you to help Carlos, did you hear me?* You've let him spill his milk! My head, it's splitting!"

She began banging the pan against the stove.

"Juanita!" George laughed. "Simmer down, baby."

Slumped on the sofa by a window with a history book in his hands, Keeny gazed out the window, gored by the rough-haired beast called Frustration. He had changed his clothes and was ready to pull out as soon as he had eaten dinner. He wore a black shirt with short sleeves, black pants, and the white nylon barber's jacket.

Beyond the window the Project houses lay heaped darkly; lighted windows gleamed behind leafless sycamores. Autos glided along the twisting roadway, seeming to sniff the pavement like hounds. Keeny chewed his lip, his nerves tangled up like fishline.

He let his mind slip out of gear.

The shrill voices of the flat came through a gentle roaring, like voices in a bus. He imagined he was on a mountainside, miles from the city. In a sort of trance, he seemed to smell pine trees and to feel on his face a clean, cool breeze. He was alone, like that dude, Thoreau, in his cabin, that he'd read about in the joint. . . .

Then hands were suddenly shaking him, and he rushed back to awareness. His mother's face, disfigured with rage, went through clownish contortions inches from his own. George stood grinning behind her, a can of beer in his hand.

"I'm talking to you, Joaquín! My God, I'm screaming at you for five minutes!" Suddenly she clenched her hair in both hands and stepped back.

"His breath! George! Smell this kid's breath! What's on his breath?"

Two-year-old Armando, who had been making paper airplanes near Keeny's feet, looked up with vague interest, his face smeared with chocolate.

George sat down on the couch beside Keeny and looked at him. "What do you mean?" George always wore Wellington boots and red-plaid shirts, playing the part of a heavy-equipment operator, though the heaviest equipment he operated, to Keeny's knowledge, was a beer-can opener.

"Glue!" cried Keeny's mother. "He's been sniffing glue! That's why he doesn't hear me!"

Rousing angrily, Keeny kicked his book across the floor. "You think I'm crazy? I don't sniff glue. That stuff will rot your brain."

But when he sniffed the air, he caught an aroma of benzine. George laughed and pointed at Armando.

"It's the baby, Juanita. He's using glue."

Snatching the twisted tube from the rug beside the little boy, Keeny's mother shook her head in bitter despair.

"Why didn't you stop him, Joaquín? *Look at the*

rug! Oh, no, you just sat there and—"

"Simmer down, baby," Georger the Forger laughed.

As the family ate dinner, Keeny counted the minutes, waiting for the others to leave so that he could catch a bus for Old Town and meet the Aztecs. But while the family got organized for blast-off, George, killing off another quick can of beer, said to Keeny:

"Looks like you'll have to take care of Armando tonight, Champ. Your mother don't want to take him out with a runny nose."

Keeny's hand flapped up. "Not me! I'm going out."

George's lumpy shoulders shrugged. "Talk to your mother about it. All I know is I got to meet Eddie and she wants to go along."

His jaw set, Keeny strode to the bedroom door. In the room, his mother was yanking Carlos' jacket up his arms as though she were a psychiatric aide putting him in restraint. Carlos, eight, was fussing. Estela stood at the mirror, spraying her black hair.

"Hey, 'Stel!" Keeny said. "Save the spray. You're staying with Armando this time. I stayed last time. I've got plans."

Estela, her thin, pretty face laughing, fogged some spray toward him. "You can't run around with the Aztecs anyway. They're a bad influence."

Keeny grinned. "Huh-uh. *I'm* the bad influence. Anyway, I'm only going to the library." Quickly he turned and crossed to the front door.

"*Joaquín!*" The terrible voice stabbed him like a knife.

Keeny clenched his fists. "*What?*" he shouted back. He continued fumbling with the bolts and latches on the door.

His mother charged from the room, waving a hairbrush. "You're staying with Armando! You don't leave this place!"

"I told you, Mom—I'm going to the library!"

"If you set foot out of here I'm calling the police! It's seven-thirty and your curfew is eight. I told you to stay away from the Aztecs! So did Mr. Baker—"

"No, he didn't. Only Gato, because he's on drugs. Can I help it if he hangs around sometimes? Anyway, I'm only going to the library."

Keeny's mother brandished the hairbrush like a hatchet. Keeny fell back. Furiously, she reset all the locks.

"Go over and sit with Armando! Help him make airplanes. So help me God, I'll call the police!"

Keeny felt a tightness behind the ears, a cold breathlessness. There was a silent screaming in his head. Suddenly he kicked the door, then crossed the room and dropped onto the sofa, breathing hard. His mother followed, crying at him that she had had all she could stand, she was going to call Mr. Baker. . . .

"Call him! Okay!" Keeny yelled. "I'm staying, okay? Okay if I stay?"

George watched them, doing the silent laugh he had, a deep heaving of the shoulders without a sound coming from his mouth. Armando began to cry.

"Okay, babe, let's split," George said.

"Oh, my God," said Keeny's mother, weakly. "This parolee of mine, this *bato loco*, this glue-sniffer—"

Chapter 3

Painstakingly, Armando folded another sheet of newspaper into a limp-winged glider. He stood at the window and pushed it out into the night. The dark wind whirled the triangle of paper away. Armando leaned out to watch the glider float down.

Keeny saw him and uttered a shout. "Hey! Get back from there!"

Startled, Armando stepped back, then sat on the floor and began to cry. Keeny went to one knee beside him.

"I'm sorry, 'Mando. But you might fall. Stay back!"

Armando wailed. Finally he sobbed, "Mama said I could!"

"She didn't say you could do a nose dive from the window. You want to dive two stories onto your nose, huh?"

He tickled the little boy and Armando laughed. But when he was finished laughing, he started crying again. With a sigh, Keeny recognized the symptoms of terminal fatigue.

"Hey, let's go to bed and I'll tell you a story. Okay?"

Armando kept crying. *Brother!* Keeny thought. Wouldn't go to bed, wouldn't stop crying. He started making a new plane, while Armando, watching through tears, his nose running, continued to wail.

Keeny sailed it to him. Armando let it lie on the floor, and bawled.

"I'll make you some toast," Keeny said. "What do you want on it?"

Armando sniffled. "Sugar on it."

Keeny rumpled his curly brown hair and went to the kitchen. *Man!* The toaster was broken, so he speared a fork into the edge of a piece of bread and held it over a gas burner. When the bread was toasted, he buttered it, sprinkled it with sugar, and carried it back to the living room. Armando had wandered away. Keeny walked to the bedroom. But he was not in the bed he shared with Carlos and Keeny, and Keeny looked into the bathroom.

"Hey, *chaparro!*"

No answer: He turned on the light. The bathroom was empty. Then, from somewhere, Keeny heard a woman's voice shrilly crying out.

Shock hit him like a bullet, sudden and numbing. He dropped the toast and ran to the other room. Voices rose through the open window.

"*Dios mío! Is he dead?*"

"What is it?" a man shouted. "*What happened?*"

The paper airplane was gone from the floor. Keeny shivered. He stared in horror at the open window. The voices grew in volume. In panic, he turned to the door and started fumbling at the locks. He made himself promises.

If he's all right, I'll never be mean to him again. If he's alive, I'll go to church. I'll give up the Aztecs.

He threw the door open. Outside, there was a narrow balcony running from one end of the building to the other. The structure was really double—twin blocks of flats stacked three high like the layers of a cake, and joined in the middle by the broad open-air landings of a central stairway. On these landings were stored overflowing trash barrels and dozens of wheel-toys.

Keeny ran to the landing and started down, stumbling on the iron treads and gasping out a prayer. *"Padre Nuestro que estás en el cielo, sanctificado sea Tu nombre. . . ."* At the bottom he emerged onto a narrow path that curled through the Project like a snail's trail. Just around the corner of the building was the spot where Armando had fallen. He heard men and women calling from windows and saw others hurrying up the path.

Then he heard a child crying, and he moaned with relief.

The first thing he saw when he turned the corner was a group of Project people on the grass beside the walk. Some were kneeling; others formed a loose half-circle near the shrubbery at the base of the building. The voice of Mrs. Ortega, the neighbor below Keeny's flat, came over the child's weak cries.

"Carry him inside. The night air is bad for him!"

"No, no. . . . Don't move him," a man said.

A match was struck for a cigarette, and Mr. Ortega's face was lighted dramatically. "I called the police, but where are they ever when you need them?"

Keeny pushed through the circle. Armando lay on his back on the grass, crying feebly. One arm was flung out at a queer angle. Going to his knees beside him, Keeny patted his hand.

"Hey, 'Mando! You'll be okay. Lie still—"

Far away he heard a siren, then another and another, signaling to each other like animals in a jungle. Armando fussed almost disinterestedly.

"His arm is broken!" cried Mrs. Ortega, a small woman with black hair worn in a long pony tail. "Maybe his back is broken! He hasn't moved."

"Can you move, 'Mando?" Keeny asked. Everyone crowded closer to stare down at Armando. He lay there pale as tallow, without moving. Keeny, trying to pray, heard Mrs. Ortega whispering:

"It's the mother's fault! She should have known better than to leave him with such a boy."

Keeny looked up in resentment. "I was making him some toast, Mrs. Ortega. He wouldn't stay away from the window."

"Then why didn't you close it?"

"I—I didn't have time."

Mrs. Ortega dismissed this with a gesture of contempt.

Keeny heard a siren reach a high note and hold it. Desperately he began fitting together phrases in his mind, excuses he would need when the Man arrived.

"They were fighting all evening," Mr. Ortega was telling the others in a conspiratorial tone. "This one didn't want to stay home. He has these gang-friends—"

"Maybe he pushed him out!" said his wife.

People looked at each other, and a woman placed both hands over her mouth in horror. Keeny rose angrily. Mrs. Ortega backed up, her husband moving quickly between her and Keeny.

"Why do you want to say that?" Keeny demanded, gesturing with both hands. "What do you know about it?"

"What do we know about it?" said Mr. Ortega. "We live downstairs, don't we? We hear every word you people say, more's the pity."

"He has no natural feelings, that boy," said his wife. "He's been in prison half his life. With my three girls, I have no protection against him."

"He was sailing planes from the window," Keeny argued. "I told him not to. Then—"

The shadows reddened as a police car arrived at the point where the sidewalk emerged from the Project. Two officers, their white helmets gleaming with

25

red highlights, came at a trot with a jingle of official hardware.

The officers shone flashlights on Armando. Then one ran back to the car. Keeny saw two more police cars arrive, one of them a station-wagon ambulance. The other officer asked who Armando was, but when Keeny tried to explain, Mrs. Ortega outyelled him.

"His own brother! He pushed him out the window!"

The officer stared at Keeny as some other policemen ran up. "What's your name?" he demanded.

"Durán, Joaquín. He was sailing planes from the window and he fell out. She's lying! I didn't push him!"

Two officers came up with a wheeled stretcher. They placed it beside Armando and began discussing how to move him. Keeny fought back the tears. His face was trying to break up and he struggled to control it. An officer led him to the corner of the building.

"Where's your I.D.?" he asked.

"It's upstairs."

"All right, what happened?"

Keeny told the story again.

"Why didn't you close the window?" the officer asked.

"I didn't have time—I didn't think—"

"The lady over there says you and your brother'd been fighting."

"She's lying! He was only crying. He was tired."

The officer drilled his flashlight into Keeny's eyes and checked his pupils. Then he made him roll up his sleeves and searched for needle marks. He saw the eagle-and-serpent tattoo on Keeny's right forearm. Keeny had made it himself, with a needle and ink, in Deuell. Below the eagle were the words: *VIVA LA RAZA!*

"Are you geezing?" asked the officer.

"No, sir. I don't use anything."

"How long have you been out?"

"Six months."

"From where?"

"Deuell."

"For what?"

"Possession and—uh—assault. But see, when they busted me—"

Another policeman moved in and began writing in a notebook. He said quietly:

"The lady says she heard a loud thump on the floor. She lives downstairs. She thinks the brother knocked him down and the boy may have staggered to the window and fallen out—

"He cops out to possession and assaulting a police officer," said the other. "We'd better take him in and get a make. He's an old-timer." He reached for his handcuffs.

Keeny thought sharp and hard. When he knew a situation had gone to hell, he was usually able to free his mind from his fear and think clearly. After a moment he said, "I'll show you where it happened. I can prove it. There's an airplane on the floor where he was sailing them."

"We'd better have a look," one officer told the other.

You'd better stay straight, Keeny, Mr. Baker, his P.O. had said in his office the first day he was out. *Next time it will be Travis.* Travis was the San Quentin of Youth Authority institutions.

Okay, Mr. Baker, Keeny thought bitterly. *I tried to be a straight arrow, didn't I? But, man, how do you do it with a crazy mother, and the neighbors down on you? Man, it's not possible.*

Since he had left the door open, getting in was no problem. It required three keys to enter the flat, and

27

you couldn't even get out in less than a minute. Keeny moved a few feet into the room and pointed toward the window.

"He was playing over there. I brought him back to the middle of the rug. Then I went to make him some toast."

"Why didn't you close the window?"

"I didn't think, man! I just didn't think."

The officers nosed around the room. They were like some kind of blue-steel machine, rigid and unwieldy. The equipment they had to carry creaked and jingled: belts, handcuffs, keys, gun, badge. It made them stiff and slow, and, Keeny knew, they were about as flexible as a pistol in their thinking.

Nobody would ever convince them that he had not caused Armando to fall out the window. That was already settled. Case closed.

"Where's the airplane you said was by the window?" one of the officers asked. He had hard brown features, a tight mouth, and cool blue eyes.

Keeny blinked. "I guess he was sailing it when he fell out."

"You guess?"

The other man looked into the kitchen, then came back. He winked at his partner.

"What'd you do with the toast you made him, sport?" he asked.

Keeny frowned and scratched his head. Then he snapped his fingers. "In the bedroom. I dropped it when I heard him crying."

The policeman walked into the bedroom. The other moved to the window and looked out. Keeny took three steps backward and was out the door and on the balcony. Quietly he closed the door. The locks went home with a dry trigger-snapping. Keeny raced down the stairs, shivering with excitement and fear.

Chapter 4

The crowd was breaking up. Armando had been carried away. Keeny saw the ambulance leaving. There were police all over the place, now. An officer was looking at one of Armando's paper airplanes; another was taking a statement from the Ortegas. Coolly, Keeny turned and walked away. When he reached the end of the long Project building, he heard a shout from upstairs.

"The Durán kid— Stop him!"

Moving fast, he reached the corner of the building and ducked around it. Then he began to run, not in panic but with the steady high-striding power of a long-distance runner. He vaulted toys in his path, swerved around gas meters, dodged trees. He caught supper smells, heard television sets blaring and voices from downstairs flats. There was no great hurry now —no one around here would fink on a fugitive except a *bruja* like Mrs. Ortega—but his time-squeeze involved catching a bus. One passed every fifteen minutes on Arroyo Street, the busy avenue a few blocks away. Soon, however, police cars would be cruising every street and alley in Happy Valley. Getting on a bus would be largely luck. And while he had had a lot of luck in his life, most of it had been bad.

He pulled off the white jacket, rolled it under his arm, and took off for Arroyo Street.

When he reached the busy street, he stopped and gazed at the late evening traffic skimming along. On the near side of the street were small shops and vacant lots. Every wall was decorated with the names of kids and gangs. Across the street was a skinny belt of grass and trees called Arroyo Park. There was a bus stop over there where the street he had come in on dead-ended.

Walking like any other citizen, swinging the Mexican coin on its chain, he worked his way through the traffic. At the curb, he peered east and west. No buses in sight.

He crossed the grass of the little park to a teeter-totter and lay down on it, the jacket beneath him.

In a moment a car came down the side street to the dead end at Arroyo. He saw a dome-light on it, a tall aerial whipping. He tried to press himself into the plank, to become part of it. The police car turned west on Arroyo, then came to a squealing halt at the bus stop. An officer leaned out the window on the passenger's side and snapped on a hand-spot. The chalk-white beam seared a path across the grass, illuminating briefly and startlingly the swings, barrels, sandpiles, and teeter-totter.

Keeny's breath hissed through his teeth.

A moment later, to his astonishment, the light faded. The cruiser gunned away. His dark clothing had saved him.

Sergeant Thomas Rock, Juvenile Division commander at Chicago Street Police Station, was fielding a psycho call when the police radio brought the news about Keeny.

"I didn't get that, Mrs. Henry," he said into the telephone. "Oh, Mrs. *Enriquez*. Yes, ma'am, I remember talking to you last week. A jet plane has landed on your roof and the pilot is coming in the window! Mrs. Enriquez, that's terrible! What would you like us to do?"

He rolled his eyes up at the ceiling while the receiver crackled. The commander was a big, clean-cut man over six feet tall. He had a long, pallid face and a brush of light brown hair streaked with gray. He wore a gray business suit, but the word *cop* was chiseled into his bony features like a name on a tombstone. He listened with thinning patience. It was funny, sad, and monotonous. Every week, she called. Every week!

"Yes, I suppose we can send a car over," he said thoughtfully. "How about Easter Sunday? Well, I don't see how we can do it any earlier, Mrs. Enriquez. I'll tell you what, I'm going to transfer you to our Low-Flying Aircraft Division. They're set up to handle this kind of problem better than we are. . . ."

He punched a button and hung up.

It sometimes seemed to the sergeant that all of Dogtown was one huge pressure cooker creaking and boiling with wild, steaming craziness. Psychos setting fire to themselves, threatening to bomb churches, fighting with knives and pistols, chanting from the Bible in the parks, taking off their clothes in public. And all this terrible stuff eventually jamming into the safety valve of the pressure cooker—the Chicago Street Police Station.

Yet most of these types made little trouble for Sergeant Rock personally. The hospitals handled the majority of such cases. The ones that gave Sergeant Rock and his juvenile officers trouble were the hard-core delinquent kids—the gang-fighters, drug addicts, car-thieves, Little League burglars, cop-assaulters, killers. Day and night they freaked about the black ghettos and the Mexican-American *barrios*. Hundreds of them didn't even go to school. They passed their time leaning against lamp posts, trying to decide what delinquent act to perform next.

Sergeant Rock picked up some day-watch reports from his desk and carried them into the coffee room. Here a half-dozen officers were writing up reports at long desks like picnic tables. A trusty, sad-eyed and middle-aged, with a pouched yellow face, was making coffee in a percolator. The sergeant did not remember him. As he drew a cup of coffee, he said, "How long will we be favored with your presence?"

"Sixty-two days, Sergeant."

"More?"

"Yeah. More," the trusty said.

The sergeant dropped a nickel in an old bus fare box for his coffee and sat down. A moment later the sneak box—a radio on a desk near the door—came on with a rasp of static.

"Thirteen-L-Twenty. We've got a possible homicide. Is there a want or a warrant on Durán, Joaquín, a juvenile?"

Rock immediately went over and stood near the radio. He began to hum, his face sharpening. Durán! Homicide! He could give them the whole picture on Durán. The boy had been in Rock's life ever since the sergeant came to Chicago Street five years ago.

"No want, no warrant," a woman's voice told the officer who had called from the field.

The sergeant picked up a telephone and punched a button.

"Have Matheny call me land-line as soon as he can," he said. Land-line was a telephone. He wanted the full story on Durán before they brought him in. Possible homicide! It was likely that Durán, if he had crossed the line into homicide country, would be tried as an adult this time.

But before Officer Matheny could call in, another car radioed to the station.

"Thirteen-Zebra-Nine. Suspect now at large. Probably still in the area. Request assistance."

Sergeant Rock swore under his breath.

"All units on Thirteen," came the voice of the policewoman downstairs. "A seventeen-year-old male suspect, Mexican ancestry, wearing dark jeans and tee shirt and a white barber's jacket. Tattoo of an eagle and serpent on right forearm—"

The sergeant took a swig of coffee and handed the cup back to the trusty. "Get the dope from Matheny when he calls," he said to another officer. "I know the crowd this Durán kid hangs in with, and I'll check some of their hangouts. Tell Matheny nice going. Judas!"

Rock went back to his office for his hat. Assault to commit murder! Yet he was puzzled, because with all the raps against him, Durán had never pulled any real violence. In fact, something in the boy had intrigued him from the first, some quality that in no way matched his record. Of course, a boy *was* his record. He was not what he conned you into thinking he was; he was what he *did*.

Between Durán's outbreaks of car-stealing, burglary, and the like, however, he went to school and stayed out of trouble. Then, for no apparent reason, he would break out in a crime-rash again, like a kid coming down with the measles.

Rock got the key to a police cruiser and walked outside. The police station was a brand-new structure of shining blue tile and glass. Natives called it the Glass House. A block up the street was the old station, boarded up, now. In many ways, Rock preferred it. It was like an old, solidly built home festooned with memories. Sometimes he went up there and sniffed around the old offices and looked at the yellowing charts.

After starting the car, he turned on the radio. A woman's voice was giving Keeny Durán's description again, hitting hard on his tattoo.

It occurred to Sergeant Rock that much of Durán's trouble tied in with that Mexicanism of his: He had eagles and serpents tattooed on his brain. He wouldn't settle for being an American citizen: No, no, *he* was a *chicano!* The only instance of violence in his file had involved an arresting officer's calling him a greaser.

According to the report, the officer had stated: "Unless you get in the car, Joaquín, I will be forced to employ a sleeper hold on you."

When Rock kidded him about it, the officer admitted he had used a little profanity, had lost his temper and called Durán a greaser.

Maybe the trouble was his lousy home, Rock reflected. That hysterical mother of his! Many a time she had sat in the office and begged the sergeant to throw the book at her boy—he was beyond control, he was bad! No, the home wasn't much. But, hell. If you were going to free every felon with a bad home background, the jails would be ninety-nine percent empty tomorrow. And full again the day after. Keeny was stuck with that home like he was with his black hair and brown skin.

And now an attempted-murder rap coming up! He wondered what had happened. He wondered whether Durán was armed.

Chapter 5

Keeny rode the bus over the lumpy hills toward Chicago Street, heart of the Dogtown area. Dogtown was what they called the vast complex of ghettos, black and brown, of which Happy Valley was one. At Chicago Street, he dropped off and sat on the bus bench, his muscles locked in anxiety. Now he had to wait for an L bus to Old Town. Only four blocks west was the new Chicago Street Police Station. The street blinked and burned with neon signs on dingy buildings. There were Mexican and Japanese restaurants, black cafés featuring soul food, a Turkish bath, and the new and the old police stations. He wished he had a jacket, for the jeans and dark tee shirt were a giveaway. He had to carry the white jacket until he could dump it somewhere. Police cars passed frequently, roving to and from the station like ants about a nest. But none of them paid him the slightest attention.

A black woman on the bench was looking at him. He smiled and she looked away. Something huge, intimidating, and gaseous swerved up to the curb. But it was only the L bus, roaring in like Gangbusters. He got up and started to dart inside, then let the lady enter ahead of him. He waited, with pulse thudding, while the driver studied him. Had he already been alerted by the police? Keeny dropped three dimes in the fare box.

He took a place in back. An inexpressible loneliness settled on him, like a weight. If he could just tell somebody how it really was! But who, on this bus or anywhere else, cared how it was with Keeny Durán? For everybody was sealed in his own little coffin.

He began noticing the other passengers. A man ahead of him had a terrible, fleshy growth on the back of his neck, as big as a grapefruit. Keeny shuddered. A woman across the aisle was so fat that her body overflowed the seat like dough. There was a blind man with an aluminum shepherd's crook. The blank faces of other passengers were like masks, but he knew that behind them were secret worries about money, health, jobs, love.

Cautiously, he stuffed his white barber's jacket down behind the back seat. *All these unhappy, nervous dudes,* he thought, *and all of them wearing a front like they didn't have nerves or anxieties. Why? Why not cop out to their problems? Blow off some steam?* He wanted to stand up on the seat and yell:

Hey, you people! Anybody on a bummer like me? Let's rap about it. Everybody that needs help, get off at the next stop and we'll rap. Maybe we can't help each other, but it'd help just to know somebody else is hurting too, wouldn't it?

But he did not stand on the seat, and his worries only thickened like gravy as the bus rumbled on with its cargo of mummies.

The bus ran out onto the long bridge across the dry Angelus River, deep, dark, a half-mile broad, and lined with concrete. Down the middle of the riverbed, drowned in darkness, ran a deep slot that carried a trickle of water. Beside it a giant loom of railroad tracks gleamed darkly, sprinkled with ruby and emerald track-lights.

Near the railroad station he left the bus and walked up a dark street toward Old Town. In this section the streets crisscrossed at odd angles. Even the little

Plaza, heart of Old Town, was of an indescribable shape, like a rectangle of dough that had gone through a wringer. Shivering, Keeny reached the Plaza and looked it over like an animal on the watch for enemies.

The Aztecs might be here, killing their boredom with horseplay; or they might be down Plaza Alley, a street that took off here, ran a block, and ended at the railroad station. In the little park he saw bums sleeping on benches under shaggy old eucalyptus trees. Two winos shuffled by, treasuring the mysterious paper bags which were their trademark as a doctor's black bag was his.

But no Aztecs.

A police car passed slowly. He stood motionless, leaning against a tree. When it had cruised on, he crossed toward Plaza Alley. Closed to traffic, the alley was a tourist trap where Mexican food and imports were sold in tiny shops. Stores lined the way and stands were set up in the middle of the alley. People strolled along, eating food from waxed paper and carrying purchases. As he walked, savoring the smells of charcoal smoke and Mexican cooking, Keeny's gaze suddenly locked on a group of boys gathered around a wishing well.

His spirits lifted as he recognized his friends.

He dodged along through the crowd. The boys at the wishing well did not see him coming. A noisy dispute was taking place between six Royal Aztecs and a middle-aged man who stood in the doorway of a candle shop. The man was shouting, the boys were laughing, as they surrounded the wishing well, a raised well-ring of adobe bricks with a shingled roof and a chicken-wire grating to keep thieves from stealing the coins on the tile floor of the well.

"The coins are for the poor!" cried the shopkeeper.

"*Batos locos,* get away from there!"

Pelón, a tall boy, lean but broad-shouldered in a dark cotton shirt and tight pants, gestured with a small archer's bow he held. In the hands of Apache, another of the boys, Keeny saw an arrow with a suction-cup tip that went with the bow.

"I dropped my St. Christopher's medal in the well, old man," Pelón argued. "I swear that's all we're trying to get."

Giggling, Apache worked the rubber tip of the arrow through the chicken wire, probing down into the shallow water. His black hair was worn in a high Mohawk cut. Raising a dripping quarter from the well, he inspected it solemnly.

"No, man, that ain't it. That's only money," he said, pretending to throw the coin back but palming it. "Well, try again, huh?"

The candlemaker ventured out, shaking one fist at them. "Get away or I'll call the police."

Pelón, holding in his laughter, went to explain to the man. "Man, you don't understand. That medal protects my *life* when I travel. I'm on the road a lot, man, and if I lost it, I'd get wasted—just like that."

Keeny, close behind him now, muttered: "You're gonna get wasted right now, Pelón, if you don't knock it off. I got problems."

Pelón looked at him, first in surprise, then in concern. He had dark skin and squinting happy eyes. Tough as horsehair, his hair grew closely around the sides of his face.

"*Qué pasó?*" he asked.

"I've got to get off the street. Got your car?"

"*Sí, hombre.*"

Pelón spoke to Apache, who was drawing up another coin. Apache threw the arrow aside. Pelón told the proprietor, "Well, man, if you won't trust us. . . .

But I hope I never reach the point where I don't trust people. That's terrible."

They strung off up the street toward the Plaza. In addition to Pelón and Apache, there were Mousie, Goyo, Benny, and Gato. Keeny saw that Gato, who used hard drugs, was wired up. He was chuckling as he jingled some coins in his hand; his bearing was the boundlessly optimistic air of one high on heroin.

Suddenly Keeny gripped Pelón's arm. He was staring into the window of a small clothing store with a display of traditional Mexican garments. He had got rid of the barber's jacket; but the cops would expect that. They would be looking now for a boy in a black shirt and pants.

"How much money have you got?" Keeny asked, gazing at a red poncho with a black cactus plant worked into the front of it. A card on the poncho said: $6.00.

Pelón pulled some change from his pocket. "How much you need?" he asked.

"Six bucks. I've got about a buck."

Pelón spoke to the others, who began digging up coins they had stolen from the wishing well. Pelón collected some money and handed it to Keeny.

"That's about five," he said.

"Wait for me. If you see the Man, send somebody in. Fast."

The shopkeeper brought the red poncho from the window and Keeny pulled it on. Looking in the mirror, he liked the old-country look of himself, his nose thin and straight, his black eyes faintly Oriental. He could see himself astride a white horse, carrying a rifle at the head of a revolutionary army. . . .

"Okay. I'll wear it," he said.

He started counting out quarters. The boy called Mousie, an expression of alarm on his face, entered the shop. His real name was Mickey, for Miguel; from there it was just a step to Mousie. Mousie's mind was slow, partly because he kept it dazed with so many of the red pills called downers.

"The Rock's coming, Keeny!" whispered Mousie.

Keeny's heart squeezed but he kept counting coins onto the shopkeeper's palm. "Where from?"

"The Plaza." Mousie kept his hand over his mouth. When he spoke, he made his fingers flop like the broken wing of a bird. It was only one of several strange things about him.

Keeny thought of escape routes. There was no rear entrance to the shop, he knew, for all the buildings backed up to a chain-link fence topped with barbed wire, and beyond the wire a blank brick wall rose from the ground. The only way out was the way he had come in. Of all the cops in town, he feared Sergeant Rock most, for the Rock was not only smart, but had accepted Keeny as his personal cross. His aim was to see him locked up finally and forever as an habitual criminal.

"I'll get you tried as an adult, Durán," he had promised Keeny last time. "And they'll throw away the key."

Keeny stood by the door. He saw the Aztecs huddled nervously before the shop, gazing toward the Plaza. Keeny followed their gaze but did not see the Rock. He went out and stood beside Pelón. Pelón gestured with his thumb.

"He went inside that restaurant. What's happening, man?"

"A bad scene at home. Where's your car?"

"At the Plaza. We'll have to leave by the other end of the alley and circle back."

Keeny jarred him with his elbow and started down the alley, weaving through the crowd, keeping behind the stands in the middle of the alley. Suddenly he saw a blue uniform a hundred feet ahead. He swore under his breath and halted. The officer was sauntering up, swinging a nightstick, from the lower end of the alley. The other boys halted, too, as Keeny, desperate, looked about for a hiding place.

They had stopped before a small café with a half-height wall which could be shuttered at night; inside, there was a little dining room with a half-dozen tiny square tables in it. Keeny saw a stout Mexican lady and an old man wearing a dishwasher's cap puttering about the kitchen. The kitchen was about the size of a bathroom.

"Come on!" he said, and started into the restaurant.

Pelón hung back. "Man, it's too small! You'll stick out like a fly on a wall."

Keeny walked inside. The restaurant was warm, fragrant of chili and onions. He pulled two of the little tables together on the brick floor so that they could all sit down. The Aztecs sat, dazed with anxiety. Keeny's mind began to work. The fat lady came to the counter that divided the kitchen from the dining room and smiled at the boys.

"*Buenas noches, señora,*" Keeny said affably. "We would like six tacos, please."

The woman turned away. Keeny heard hot grease sputter as tortillas were dropped into it. But in a moment the woman returned.

"Excuse me, *joven,* there are seven of you."

Grinning, Keeny got up. "*Sí, Señora.*" He went behind the counter into the kitchen. There was a greasy gas stove, a stained sink, a work table on which rested pans of grated goat's cheese, onions, lettuce, and tortillas.

"We have here," he said, in elegant Spanish, "a young man who needs a job for a few minutes. Perhaps he could wash dishes. He is not proud and he is a good worker."

The old man at the sink glowered at him. "That's *my* job, boy."

"But its just for a few minutes, *viejo*. I'll work free. Here, let me have that greasy platter. I'll have it so clean you could eat off it."

"Well, that's what it's for," said the old man. "They look like troublemakers to me, Guadalupe—"

Keeny appealed to the woman. "One *chicano* for another, eh, *señora?*"

The woman smiled. "Let him wash the dishes," she told the old man. "You can grate some more cheese while he's here."

"A beautiful lady like you," said Keeny, "I knew you wouldn't turn a poor young man away." He was not fooling her. But she was one who knew that anywhere you sliced the *barrio,* it bled trouble. Some people would help, some were too deep in their own troubles to care.

With a laugh, the woman put the old man's white cap on Keeny's head.

Five minutes later, as he was scrubbing a greasy pan with a scouring pad, Keeny heard a familiar baritone voice outside the taco shop.

"Hello, hello! If it isn't the Royal Aztecs! What are you dudes up to? Having lion-meat enchiladas, or whatever royal warriors like you eat?"

Keeny kept scrubbing. He heard Pelón's mournful voice reply:

"Just rapping, Sergeant Rock, just rapping. How are you, Sergeant?"

"Just right, Pelón. I'll have a cup of coffee and rap along with you."

Chapter 6

"Short a couple of members tonight, aren't you?" said the sergeant. "Where's Little Apache and Duck Lips?"

Keeny, his back to the eating area, knew from the force with which his voice carried that the Rock was facing the kitchen. He imagined him in his gray suit and snappy hat, pale and smiling.

Gato's voice said cheerfully: "Little Apache's going with a girl over in the Hole. And Duck Lips got busted last month in San Diego."

"That's right, I forgot. Two hundred pounds of weed in his gas tank or something, wasn't it?"

"Under the hood," said Gato. "Just two kilos. It was a bummer, though. He didn't know it was there. Somebody stashed it while he was having dinner. He was really as clean as I am, Sergeant."

Shut up, fool! thought Keeny. *In a minute he'll want to look at your arms.*

"Every bit, I'm sure," said the officer. "Your brother," he said to Apache, "would do himself a favor by staying out of the Hole. A National Geographic team is in there right now, looking for headshrinkers. Little Apache has no fighting gang to back him up, and that girl, Yo-Yo, has a brother in the Cobras. Little Apache will be lucky to get out of that love affair alive. Unless you Cub Scouts consider yourselves a fighting gang?"

Out of the corner of his eye, Keeny saw the uniformed officer come to the half-height wall of the café and gaze in, revealing no recognition even of the sergeant. He tapped once on the wall with his nightstick and sauntered on. Keeny's knees quaked.

"No, sir, we aren't a gang," mumbled Mousie. "We're just a group."

"Exactly, Mousie! And as long as you understand that, you're safe. But if you dudes ever get classified as a gang, every one of you that's on probation or parole will get busted. Oh, and what about Keeny Durán?" asked the sergeant. "I don't see him."

Keeny swallowed a lump the size of a scouring pad.

"Keeny?" several boys said at once.

"You know. The good-looking boy with the tattoo. He was wearing a dark tee shirt, black pants, and that white barber's jacket tonight when he pushed his brother out of the window."

All of the boys expressed amazement, and Gato said he would come down to the station right now and give a character reference for Keeny if it would help prove that he hadn't done it.

The sergeant shed his friendliness like a snakeskin.

"Shut up, Gato. If I take you down to the station, it won't be because of your fine character, it'll be to give you a Nalline test. *Where is he?*" His voice hit out like a fist.

The boys said they had not seen him. Keeny heard a table creak as the Rock leaned on it.

"All right, then. If he cops out that he was with you tonight, I'll see that every one of you gets revoked. That'll mean hard time for one or two of you. Now, are you sure you don't know anything about him? In a general, non-fink way?"

Pelón said, "If he was home, Sergeant, and we were over here, how could we know where he is now?"

"How long have you been here?"

"Couple of hours."

"Where's your car parked?"

"Up at the Plaza."

"I'll feel the radiator when I leave. If it's hot, I'm taking you all in for questioning. Durán's gone bigtime, and we want him. *Nos huachamos!*"

Keeny heard the Rock's chair scrape as he got up. He tried to swallow, but his tongue was pasted to the roof of his mouth like a Band-Aid. He made a gulping noise.

He heard a jingle of keys and coins as the sergeant walked out.

The woman served the tacos. The boys took a long time eating them. Pelón came to the counter and tapped a coin on it. "I guess that's all, *señora.*"

Keeny turned. Pelón's black eyes, with scars in the brows, were sad. "What do you say?" he asked Keeny, softly.

"Take off, *comarado.* We'll never get out of here together. They'll follow you anyway."

"What will you do?"

"I'll sleep someplace tonight. Tomorrow I'll go over to Rosie's and see if I can get a bed there for a while." Rosie's was the old snake-den boardinghouse that had been closed.

"Man, good luck," Pelón said, and they gripped in the secret *chicano* way. "You know, man, if you come out of the joint and get busted again before you get the free feeling—well, man, it ain't that bad going back. There's nothing to it. Maybe you ought to telephone the Rock and get points for attitude."

"I been out too long," Keeny said. "I've already got the feeling, Pelón. I had the feeling I was going places, too, but they don't give you a damn chance."

He could tell from Pelón's expression that he did not get that shot, about going someplace. Going where? Just like on the bus tonight, nobody ever really knew what you were thinking. Everybody lived in his own little fishbowl.

Pelón paid for the tacos, then gave Keeny some more quarters from the wishing well.

"Listen," Keeny said suddenly, "be at the taco stand across from school at three-thirty. I'll call you at the telephone booth. Find out how my brother is. I'm afraid to telephone the hospital. They might trace the call."

The woman let Keeny stay for a while in the café, drinking coffee at one of the crazy-legged tables. The tourists were thinning out. Keeny did not want to be the last to leave Plaza Alley, so, seeing a Mexican family departing, he attached himself to them as closely as he dared, trying to look like the big brother of the four small children. The father and mother gave him some curious glances, at which Keeny would smile and nod.

At the Plaza, before leaving the alley, he sniffed the night. A damp mist of smog muted the lights. Cars hummed past. Down Angelus Street he saw the red tail-lights of autos submerging into Skid Row.

He decided to try to make it to an all-night theater on Skid Row. He began walking.

Six blocks west, a grimy area began. There were bars with entrances as forbidding as sewer manholes, flophouse hotels—BED AND TOWEL 50¢—pawnshops, peep shows, and girlie theaters. He dodged winos steering their way painstakingly down sidewalks that despite all their pains, usually led straight to the drunk tank. Passing a midnight mission, he hesitated a second, then turned in.

The huge room was full of men, many in overcoats, watching television or playing cards and dominoes.

Under some stairs at one side, a small trade in old shoes was taking place. He remembered, then, being here once: It was called the In-Jesus-Name-Amen Rescue Mission, but was purely a recreation hall. You could get a shower, DDT for your lice, and stay out of the weather until ten o'clock. But no beds. You had to find a flop at another mission.

He left. A police car passed on cat's feet. Chewing on a hangnail, he paced on through the traffic of derelicts and freaks. An old man wearing white cotton gloves flipped up the canopy of each trash-receptacle and dived for treasure. A blind man with black glasses approached; every few seconds he would blow on a whistle. Another man, young and carrying a Bible, was attempting to cross the street. He would get only as far as the middle before ducking back to the curb, raging at an invisible barrier out there that somebody had erected to keep him from going where the Lord wanted him to go.

What kept Keeny's pulse thrumming was the knowledge that a certain number of the freaks had to be plainclothesmen. The bars were full of them. Some guy with four days' whiskers and booze-ravaged features was just as likely to step up to him with handcuffs glinting in his hands and a grin on his face.

"Let's go, Durán," he would say.

FIVE MAJOR ACTION FEATURES FIVE!

A rippling theater marquee caught his eye. He crossed the street, bought a ticket, and slipped into a blessed darkness torn by the crackle of cowboy gunshots. On the back of each seat was a white huck-towel to protect the worn-out upholstery from the greasy necks of the audience. The theater was tiny and narrow, with ornate little boxes that made him think of the theater where President Lincoln had been shot. For that matter, the picture that was showing, an old Western, might have been made in Civil War times, too.

The small audience did not respond to the picture one way or another. They were here to sleep. The film was so scratchy that it looked as though it had been filmed in a blizzard of hay. Keeny took a seat in the middle of an empty row and slumped down.

Presently another picture was on, a horror movie. Then it was a monster show. Midway through this one, Keeny fell asleep.

Chapter 7

The night passed like a fever-dream. Intervals of awareness broke the parade of hours. Twisting and turning, he tried to relieve the torture of sleeping erect. Half-waking, he would check the lighted clock on a side wall and exhaustedly sink into a coma again.

At last he was looking at the clock and it said eight o'clock. Daylight leaked in around the aisle curtains. Many of the derelicts had left. Keeny's mouth tasted leathery, and his joints ached as though he had been in a motorcycle accident.

From the theater he emerged to a damp, raw morning with fine rain driving scraps of trash down the street. He ducked into a doughnut shop where he bought four chocolate-covered doughnuts and a cup of coffee. Eating, he planned his visit to Rosie's foster home. Though she had lost her license, she probably still had her kindly, boozy old heart. Rosie would hide him for a couple of days. Getting there might be hair-raising, though, for the bus passed the Chicago Street Police Station and a few blocks beyond it he must get off and walk two blocks.

He looked at the gummy clock above the deep-fry wells: eight-thirty. With good bus connections, he could be on Rosie's street while a few kids were still hurrying to school.

Wearing the red poncho, he caught a bus to Old

Town and transferred to a Dogtown bus. On the walks, kids were hurrying to school, most of the girls wearing scarves over their heads. The fine rain had lifted, but clouds, thick and gray, scudded overhead.

Ahead, he saw the police station, a shining shoebox of blue tile and glass. The bus rolled by it. Coming up, then, was the old station house, a two-story block of grimy red brick. He remembered it well, like a school he had once gone to, his alma mater. Juvenile Division. The drinking fountain that spat in your face however you eased it on; the antiquated toilets with a wooden tank up near the ceiling and a pipe the water roared down. The trusty's cell upstairs. But the screens were dense with grime, now, and a sign on the front door said:

CLOSED. CALL AT STATION TWO BLOCKS NORTH.

At Marquette, Rosie's street, Keeny stepped down and headed quickly along the narrow street. Wind blew papers along the gutters. Quarter-sized leaves from camphor trees skidded past. Nearing Rosie's, he looked for suspicious cars. Two or three were parked in the block, all of them empty. He shot a quick glance over the house. Two stories high, it stood on stilts like a jungle dwelling and was painted the color of rat poison, a venomous blue-green. With its steep roof sloping down on all sides, it looked as though it might once have been thatched. A wild tangle of poinsettias bearing stunted red flowers flapped against the front windows. A large, shabby palm tree shook its torn fronds in the front yard with a swordlike rattling.

Keeny went to the door. The bell was a key you twisted, activating some mechanism like a bicycle bell inside the house. He rang three times. At last he heard footfalls and the door cracked open.

"Hi, Rosie!" Keeny said cheerfully.

The flaccid old face in the slot stared in suspicion. Then: "Keeny! Well, what do you know?"

With a wrench of the stomach, Keeny walked into a dark living room smelling of stale tobacco smoke breathed and re-breathed until it was rancid. All the shades were drawn, for Rosie distrusted sunlight. She closed the door and stood beaming at him.

"Well, it's so good to *see* you, sweetie!" she said, with boozy affection. She reached up and kissed him, right on the lips. Keeny wanted to boil his mouth. Rosie wore a Hawaiian sunsuit that partially revealed breasts like a spaniel's ears, a little pot belly, and tinkertoy-like legs. She suffered from a disease that had turned her skin magenta. She was a grotesque old doll, all bones, joints, and purple skin, balanced on stiltlike heels.

"Things look just the same, Rosie," Keeny said ambiguously, gazing around at the broken sofas and chairs. He remembered the parlor full of parolees, most of them loaded on drugs or wine. Weird conversations would be going on. A boy and a girl would lie on a sofa practically doing it. Rosie would come out of the kitchen with a drink and a cigarette in one hand, and say:

"Hell, I burned the spaghetti. Help yourself, anybody that wants dinner."

Old home week.

"Had a feeling I'd see you today," said Rosie. "Hee, hee, hee!"

"How come?"

"A couple of juvenile dicks were here asking about you last night. What you been up to now, you little devil?"

Keeny grinned. "Nothing, Rosie. I was framed."

Rosie laughed again—"Hee, hee, hee!"—then began

coughing and grabbed a chairback to steady herself. Her laughter always brought on a bronchial crisis.

"Come on in the kitchen," she wheezed, after she had recovered. "I'll make you some instant."

The kitchen was filthy. Scraps of old canned food lay about, prey to ants and gnats. The stove was an inch thick with grease. Rosie put water on to boil, spooned some powdered coffee into cups, then poured whiskey into a glass and offered it to Keeny.

"No, thanks," he said.

Rosie sipped the whiskey. "I sure miss my kids," she said with melancholy. "The place is like a morgue."

Ain't it so, Keeny thought.

"I hated to lose them kids," Rosie added. "They were just like my own little boys and girls."

Keeny grinned. . . . But her little girls were always getting pregnant, and her little boys hid drugs around and got into all kinds of mischief. So they closed her down. . . . And where were all the kids now? Back in the joint, most of them. Their parents wouldn't have them, and who else would board a delinquent teenager? For all its failings, Rosie's home had, no doubt, actually kept some of the kids out of serious trouble.

"I'll tell you one kid that's ready to move in again right now," he said.

"Sorry, sweetie. Those dicks will be back again. They come here all the time anyway, and sometimes they go through the house."

"How about just till tomorrow?"

Rosie shook her head. "No, hon. No can. To tell you the truth, I think there's a stakeout on the house. A guy in a panel-body truck spent the night across the street."

"He isn't there now. And they didn't see me come in, or they'd be here knocking on the door."

"Maybe he went to the gas station to use the john,"

Rosie said. "He'll be back. He looked like a hippie, but those guys, you can't tell what kind of get-up they'll be wearing. The badge always looks the same, though. Hee, hee, hee!"

Keeny knew she was right. What he did not know was where else to go. Rosie made the coffee. It was as black as molasses. She finished her whiskey and sat at the kitchen table. Keeny saw diagonal streaks of rain appearing on the window pane.

"Did any of the guys leave some clothes?" he asked.

"All I've got is what I'm wearing."

"There's some stuff, I think. Look around upstairs."

Keeny climbed the stairs to the cold, drafty second floor. There were five rooms crowded with empty beds. He went to the old corner room he had slept in. From here he could look down on the street. The rain was falling hard now. A faded-blue panel-body truck was parked across the street. He rubbed his jaw in chagrin. Damn!

Some old clothing hung in the closet. He pulled on a black plastic car-coat. On a shelf was a high-crowned, narrow-brimmed black hat, with holes in a few places. He put it on. As he was leaving, he remembered his roomy's stash-place in the closet. If Johnny had been rousted, there was no telling what he had left. The stash-place was behind the middle hinge of the closet door. Johnny had removed the screws where the hinge was anchored to the wall and excavated some wood underneath. A thumbtack kept the hinge from pulling away to reveal the hiding place.

Keeny removed the tack and folded back the hinge. Hot dog! A couple of roaches, a kit, and at least a dozen red capsules in a small plastic bottle! He took the reds and left the kit and butts.

Downstairs, he told Rosie: "You're right. There's a

stake-out. I'll go out the other way and through the backyard. I, uh—I've got a little problem, Rosie—"

"Would two dollars help?" Rosie laughed.

"Sure would. I'll pay it back."

He had a strong yearning to drop a couple of the reds. When a scene was bad, the pills fuzzed the outlines so that you could hardly tell it from a good scene. But he couldn't chance tripping on a curb or nodding on the bus bench.

On the other hand, he had been in this bag often enough to know that the only way out of it was by the open end, where they waited. So what comes next, *chicano?*

The rain's getting to me, he thought. In some way he was going to beat them this time. He was going to make his way to Mexico—get on a freighter at the harbor—*something.* He was not going to Deuell again.

"So long, Rosie," he said. "I love you."

"You little grease-ant!" Rosie laughed.

From the back porch he surveyed a congregation of backyards. There were broken picket fences, old tires, car parts, cans, and bottles. Over the junk heaps roved subtropical plants that thrived on neglect: red cannas, poinsettias, oleanders, castor bean. Rain was beginning to drip from the eaves.

Skid Row or bust, he thought.

Chapter 8

The rain had scoured Skid Row's derelicts from the sidewalk like stains. Cold, hard drops of water shattered on the walks and glazed the street. Sparse midmorning traffic splashed along as Keeny hurried dejectedly, head down, against a wet wind toward Seventh Street. The cheapest flophouses were on Seventh, below the theater where he had spent last night. But the cops checked them, too.

Bad scene.

Then, as he passed the theater, something caused him to stop and stare. Set back out of the rain was a life-sized display dummy of a Mexican in the uniform of a revolutionary fighter. Bandoliers of ammunition crossed his chest. He wore a white sombrero, and his raised hand clutched a cardboard rifle. He had a smooth brown face with a heavy underlip, dark features that were young, and a full black longhorn mustache. But it was the eyes that had arrested Keeny—bold, light-hearted, keen.

VIVA ZAPATA! said the printing on the dummy. HE DARED A THOUSAND DEATHS TO LEAD HIS PEASANT ARMY TO GLORY!

FRIDAY THROUGH TUESDAY, a sign added.

Gooseflesh ran up Keeny's arms. The dummy's eyes drilled into his; they were like human eyes embedded in the heavy cardboard. Hunched with cold, Keeny

55

straightened. He felt like a peasant soldier brought before the great general, Emiliano Zapata, for questioning about his courage before leading a daring patrol. He felt a thrill of excitement. He wanted to humble himself before the general; then, accepted, to risk his life for him.

"'*Miliano—!*" he murmured.

The brown face smiled. *Don't be afraid, joven,* the eyes seemed to say. *Of me, or of anyone.*

Keeny looked at the figure with reverence. The peasant general wore boots with huge spurs, leather pants, a black coat hanging open. His hat was the plain white sombrero, very large, of southern Mexico. Everything about him was simple but strong. His features told of a complex mind, dashing yet cautious, capable of cruelty but always just; savage, kindly, understanding.

Keeny blew a drop of rain from his nose. All at once he shivered. For the weird idea had seized him that this facsimile of a man dead fifty years was going to speak! *Man, I've flipped out!* he thought dazedly.

Glancing around, he saw that the young woman ticket-seller was chewing gum and reading a paperback novel. Moving closer to the dummy, he whispered:

"'Miliano—camarada—it's a bad scene. What should I do?"

The mouth seemed to broaden. Keeny sensed that at any moment Zapata would speak! *Well, man, this is crazy!* he thought.

"*Qué voy a hacer?*" he asked, thinking that perhaps 'Miliano would understand Spanish better.

The dark eyes watched him. Suddenly, however, they seemed to go dead. Keeny stole another look at the box office. The ticket-seller was watching him, a girl about eighteen years old with inch-long false eyelashes and green eye makeup.

Keeny looked back again. Now it was only a cardboard dummy: lifelike, colorful, yet obviously paper. Sadly he wiped the rain from his face. Shoulders slouching, he walked on down the street.

At the corner he looked back, beseechingly. He could barely make out Zapata, his arm aloft as though to call him back.

Words formed in Keeny's head.

Hide under their noses. The least likely place—that's the place.

"Wait a minute—I don't get it—" he whispered.

The message was not repeated. Yet he would swear he had heard it!

He said to himself slowly, *The least likely place. . . .*

The way 'Miliano Zapata himself would have hidden, in the very town where enemy soldiers were quartered. But where would that be? At Rosie's?

A police car rolled by, tires hissing. The officer at the wheel did not even look at him. Keeny began to smile.

He tingled as though he had been plugged into a secret source of energy that enabled him to read 'Miliano's message: *Hide in the old police station!*

For ninety cents, Keeny bought a second-hand claw hammer at the Volunteers of America store, and a rusty cold chisel. Walking to the bus stop, he imagined that the rain blowing into his face was a warm tropical rain of southern Mexico—'Miliano's country. Emiliano Zapata! He knew he had dreamed up the whole thing. And yet . . . did the spirit of a great man live on in the blood of his descendants, his countrymen? Like the blood particles that gave his sons brown eyes and black hair? Could courage be passed

57

on? Keeny's mother had emigrated from Puebla when she was five. That was Zapata country. Maybe in Keeny's own blood. . . .

The idea was crazy. But he decided to ride it a while. Everybody was a little crazy, one of the shrinks at Deuell had told him. So be crazy in useful ways. Pick your type of insanity with care. Be the descendant of a warrior. Don't just carry a Bible around trying to cross a street; don't search for treasure in trash barrels.

The rain had darkened the bricks of the old Chicago Street Police Station to the color of blood. Standing across the street, Keeny looked it over as the bus snorted away in clouds of smoke and steam. Two blocks to his left, through the rain, he could see the new station like a block of ice. Again he studied the old station.

At the right end of the building was a covered driveway under which police cars used to unload prisoners, including Keeny Durán. Names and initials had now been spray-painted on the walls. The windows were tall, narrow, and rusty-screened, barred on the lower floor. Pipes crawled up and down the bricks like vines. Behind the building was an alley lined by shabby frame houses. At a corner of the building, beyond the covered drive, he saw an iron fire-escape ladder from the roof.

Keeny jogged across the street and up the drive. He sent one quick look along the alley before starting to climb. Cold and wet, the rungs were sharp with rust. Standing on the flat roof behind the two-foot-high parapet, he surveyed the alley below him.

All clear.

On the tarred and graveled roof were standpipes, each wearing a small rusty hat, and a little forest of sheet-metal ventilators. There was also a small, peak-roofed, windowless hut. He had never seen the hut before, but he recognized it by type: a locked stairway. It looked like a very tiny, green-roofed, railroad station.

Boldly he walked to it. The door was fastened by a laminated padlock. He smirked. He had broken into dime stores with better locks than that. With two blows of the hammer and chisel he broke the lock open. Inside the hut, he paused to re-latch the door with an old-fashioned hook-and-eye. The stairway sloped down into shadows, a door at the foot of it. He descended, took hold of the knob, and listened. Then he opened the door.

He was in the upstairs hallway. Overhead, a dusty night-light burned. In one glance he knew where he was; he could have drawn a plan of the rest of the floor.

At the alley end of the hall was Juvenile Division, the old kingdom of the Rock. Between that room and the stairs was a coffee room where the cops used to write up their reports and shoot the bull. At the far end of the hall, over the street, was a two-bunk cell for the trusties who kept the place clean and made coffee for the policemen.

He stepped into the hall. Again he listened. No reason to think there would be a full-time watchman. He guessed that a janitor or somebody came around once in a while and looked things over.

Feeling his pulse thumping in his throat, he moved down the hall. A night-light burned in the coffee room. Another glowed in the trusties' cell. On each of the two bunks lay a flabby mattress.

Returning to the coffee room, he looked things over. One of the old-style faucets had dripped until it made a river of rust down the porcelain to the drain. It told him that at least there was water. In a wooden blank-case were dusty forms of various colors. On a wall was a large city map with colored pins in it showing where certain crimes had been committed.

He went down to the cell, took off his car-coat and poncho, and lay on the mattress, grinning at the stained ceiling.

"Think I'm going to be real comfortable here, 'Miliano. Got to get a few supplies in, though. A hot plate. Canned food. A blanket or two. A Japanese transistor. Some wine."

Then reality collapsed upon him like a tent.

With sad recognition, he saw how he had deceived himself. It was just as though he had stayed on Skid Row or at Rosie's, only now he had more time to sweat. For the Rock would never call in his hounds until he had him.

The terrible aloneness he had felt on the bus closed in again. In panic he felt for the cylindrical bulge in his pants pocket and pulled out the bottle of sleeping pills. He counted out four of the shining little red bombs loaded with good feelings and trudged to the coffee room. In a cupboard he found some cups stained with coffee dregs. He let a faucet run until the rust-color left the water. He drew a cupful, dropped the capsules on his tongue, and sent them down with a drink of water.

He went back to the cell and waited for the stumblers to start turning off the lights in his skull one by one until darkness came and there was no cruel reality to face. *Nada, nada.* No reality, no problems. No nothing.

Chapter 9

Keeny went down hard, making no effort to fight the drowsiness as one did when getting loaded for kicks. He pitched headfirst into darkness and lay as one dead. Later he floated up like a waterlogged plank in a harbor. Mystified, he frowned at the bars of his cell. He reared up, flinging one hand out.

"Hey, wha'— Wha's—?"

Bad scene! How had he got here? Then he remembered. He fell back, slept again. But a forgotten duty kept plucking at his sleeve.

Call Pelón.

Lying on his back, he wriggled comfortably. Call Pelón? Why? Consciousness rose slowly, like a tide. He remembered, then, like a conversation from last year. Call Pelón at the taco stand, about Armando.

Now he sat up in alarm, made a face, and hung his head. He pressed his thumbs against his eyeballs and tried to breathe deeply, but his lungs felt paralyzed. He wrinkled his nose in self-disgust.

After a moment he looked at his watch. His vision was so blurred that he could barely read it. *Three-fifteen.* The figures rang in his head like a gong. Fifteen minutes to get sober enough to get to a telephone. And the Rock sitting two blocks away tapping his desk with a pencil and trying to dope out where Durán was hiding. . . .

He had to call, risky or not, because he needed the Aztecs' help, and this would be his only chance to contact them.

He drank some rusty water. From the window, he gazed across the roofs toward the new station house. The rain had cleared and snowy white clouds were heaped around the horizon. He stumbled downstairs to look for a safer way in and out than the roof. Beyond the empty Watch Commander's office, a short hall led to a door on the driveway. A heavy lock secured it. He retracted the bolt and turned the knob. The door opened.

He floundered upstairs in a drunken half-run, hoping the exertion would flush some blood through his clogged brain cells. He pulled on the car-coat and hat, went back downstairs, let himself out, and started up the street toward a Texaco station where there was a telephone booth.

The booth, an old green wooden frame with chicken-wire glass walls, was empty when he arrived. Keeny dropped his dime on the floor, muttering as he retrieved it from the cigarette butts and trash. He pushed it in the slot and dialed.

Pelón's voice came on the line.

"Hey, man," Keeny said hoarsely.

Pelón laughed. Keeny could hear him say to someone else, "He's loaded. Man," Pelón said, "where you at?"

"Get this," Keeny said slowly, fighting his thick tongue. "I've got a rack in the old police station."

"What do you mean? Are you busted?"

"No, the *old* station—I broke in. Have you got any bread?"

"A little, but—"

"I need some things. Did you call about Armando?"

"He's got a broken arm. They're making tests for

concussion or something, but I guess he's okay. What's the scoop? Where are you now?"

"At the Texaco station on Arroyo. Can you come tonight and bring some money?"

"*Simón*. Where at?"

"The police station. I'd better not come out again. Park a block or two away and walk. Better come one or two at a time. I'll leave the side door unlocked."

Keeny walked a half-block to a dingy counter café. He ordered a hamburger and coffee and dispiritedly gazed about. The place had a dismal religious motif. In plywood racks were some little two-inch-square paperback Bibles and tracts. On the wall hung a pencil drawing of Jesus, looking like a juvenile delinquent with beard, long hair, and loser's eyes. He attempted to read one of the Bibles, but his eyes would not focus.

Walking back to the station, he felt better, riding on the energy in the food. A police car rolled south on Chicago Street; another, cruising north, swung into the parking lot of the new station.

He hurried inside.

Shadows deepened in the old station house, settling in the corners like cobwebs. He found a bale of moldy newspapers in the basement and tried to read, but a clawing restlessness kept him pacing. He nodded on his cot for a while; when he came around, it was after seven.

The first to arrive were Pelón and Mousie. From a front window he watched them approach. He let them in and closed the door again quickly. Pelón shook him by the shoulders.

"Man, you've got to be crazy! Hiding out in a police station!"

Keeny grinned wearily. "Figure I'll open a chain of

63

old police stations for guys on the lam. Stay at a different one each night." He sent them up to the coffee room.

Apache arrived, brushing his Mohawk cut with a comb and grinning. Goyo showed up a minute later. He was a short, powerful boy whose stubby arms had curiously small hands at the ends of them; his dusty black hair was like a bear's. Keeny sent the boys upstairs.

Gato came, charged up like a warm pop bottle. Gato was tall and thin, with frail shoulders like a coat hanger under his tight jacket.

"This is great, man," he said. "But listen." Gato grew very earnest when he was on drugs. "You've got to square it with the Rock sooner or later, man. I'm just telling you for your own good."

Keeny waited, deadpan.

"You've got class, and all that crap, but you're not going nowhere till you get straightened out. Did I tell you what *I'm* going to do? I'm kicking the stuff tomorrow and enrolling in that college deal—Project Hope—where they *pay* you to go to school. I'm really gonna make something of my life."

Keeny pointed him upstairs. "Uh-huh, Gato, you're gonna make something of it, all right. A mess, the way you're going."

"Man, I was geezy for thirty days at Preston, and I never got hooked. I could quit tonight."

"Yeah, yeah," Keeny said. "Go on upstairs."

There was another tap on the door. Keeny let in Shorty Madrid, a stocky, grinning boy wearing a black knitted cap pulled down to his ears. Recently he had shaved his head while drunk. He was self-conscious about his bald skull now.

"Anybody else coming?" asked Keeny.

"No. Little Apache's with that girl over in the Hole."

The Royal Aztecs were laughing in the coffee room when Keeny and Shorty entered. All but Pelón sat at the sheet-metal-topped tables. Pelón, using his long pocket comb as a pointer, stood at the old crime-rate chart.

"Men, this is a very bad scene," he said, rapping on the chart. "Car Clout went up again in our division last month. And look what's happened to Narcotics —up eighty-seven percent! Officer Gato, are you doing your bit to stamp out narcotics?"

Gato stamped on the floor. "I'm stamping, Sergeant!"

"You still using Plan A, Officer Gato, where you shoot all the junk you find into yourself to keep the addicts from using it?"

"Still using Plan A, Sergeant!"

"Officer Apache, is your brother still on undercover assignment with the Cobras?"

"Still on undercover assignment, Sergeant. He's using the front of going with a Cobra's sister's girlfriend to observe their activities."

"Sergeant Pelón," said Keeny, "I'll take the group now."

"This whole deal is a bummer," he told them. He sat on a table facing the others. "I've been clean ever since I got out. I haven't even dropped any pills to speak of."

They all nodded. It was so.

"But once they get that sleeper hold on you, they don't turn you loose. The Rock told me last time I got busted:

" 'I'm working on a plan where hard-core repeaters

like you live on a special island. You can rob and shoot and stab each other and run your own show. There'll be special stores on the island, and when you need anything, you just steal it.'"

Frowning, the Aztecs went about their individual habits, biting nails, smoking, picking at threads in their clothes like monkeys searching for fleas.

"Well, I mean, uh, whatcha gonna do, Keeny?" Mousie asked.

"I may go the revolutionary route," Keeny said. "I'm weighing the idea. Hide out like Zapata or one of those Mexican rebel cats, and bug the cops silly."

"Who's he?" asked Goyo.

"Are you kidding? He was—" Keeny found he was not sure. He had some recollection of hearing or reading about Zapata, one of the revolutionary leaders, but it wasn't enough to hold on to. "Well, if you don't know, I don't have time to tell you. What I've got to get going on is stocking this pad with the things I need to hide out. Because I'm not turning myself in this time. What've I got to win?"

"Tha'z right!" said Gato.

"You won't believe this," said Keeny, "but I got the idea from Zapata himself!"

Pelón, combing his mustache, glanced up suspiciously. "I thought you'd come down, man. Sounds to me like you're still way up."

"I'll tell you about it while we're shopping."

Mousie, who always had money to loan if you wanted to pay his outrageous interest rate, had brought fifteen dollars for Keeny. Keeny complained about paying a dollar a week interest. Mousie shrugged.

"So pay it back sooner," he said.

Chapter 10

Most of the articles on Keeny's list could easily have been shoplifted. Stealing would have been quicker and simpler than waiting in line to check things out. But Keeny could not imagine Emiliano Zapata hiding a jar of instant coffee inside his poncho and slinking from a store. Of course, he would have stolen a railroad train with Federal supplies without batting an eye. But shoplift? Never!

He had Pelón drive to a supermarket near the river, where he shopped like any taxpayer. The Aztecs waited for him in the car. He bought food, a toothbrush, cooking utensils, and other items. He carried the sack of supplies out to the car and got in again.

"Know where the Volunteers of America store is?" he asked Pelón.

"Off Skid Row? Sure."

They drove down Angelus Street to Hancock, down Hancock to the second-hand store. Keeny purchased a used razor, a rusty hot plate, and an old army blanket. The lot came to three-seventy-five. He began to have a good, dug-in feeling, now. Pelón started the car again and they headed back to Angelus Street. He stopped for a red signal.

Keeny thought of being alone again in the old station house, and the good feeling left him. He imagined swallowing a few reds and waiting for the first wave of numbness to wash over him. Pills might be bad, but they were better than facing things you could not face.

Who are you trying to kid, Durán? he asked himself. *When you come down, it will be all the worse.* He sighed. If there were only somebody to rap to there! It was the being alone, arguing with himself, chewing on his worries until they gagged him, that he feared most.

A rippling theater marquee down the street caught his eye.

FIVE MAJOR ACTION FEATURES FIVE!

He sat up, tingling with inspiration. He could just make out Emiliano Zapata standing near the box office with his rifle raised in greeting. At the sight of the general, Keeny's spirits came up cautiously, like a whipped dog waiting to see whether it was safe to venture out. The signal changed and Pelón started to turn right. Keeny clutched his arm.

"No, man, *left!*"

"But—"

"I've got to have a *comarado* in that pad of mine. We're going to pick up a guy I can really rap to. Park this side of the Starlight Theater."

While they drove toward it, he told the boys what he wanted them to do.

Pelón parked. Keeny got out. Zapata seemed to grin at him as he walked by. A young weight lifter in a seedy blue uniform stood at the door, looking bored. No one was going in or out. The ticket-seller was chewing gum and reading her book. Keeny went on to the corner.

He heard car doors slamming. Soon the Aztecs came slouching along. They read the theater posters and laughed. Gato leaned against the box office and began talking to the girl, who looked annoyed.

The other boys wandered around, talking loudly. Finally they decided to go inside. Pelón went to the box office and spoke to Gato. But Gato shook his head.

"*I* ain't got the bread, man! I thought you had the bread."

"Man, I gave it to you!" Pelón shouted.

The giant in the blue uniform started toward them.

"No, man, look—" Gato pulled his pockets out. "*I* ain't got any bread. *You* had the bread."

Pelón shoved him. Gato shoved back. The other boys gathered around and began shoving each other. The ticket-taker came up, shoved everybody, and told them to knock it off. They argued. But foot by foot he backed them towards the car. At the car they stopped. Pelón seized the young man's arm and began appealing for fairness. The ticket-seller marked her place in the book and watched the action.

Keeny ducked behind the box office and went straight up to the general. He lifted the dummy, walked from the theater, ducked around the corner, and stood it against the wall. An hour seemed to pass before he heard the car coming, coughing in its bronchial way. There were no outraged shouts from the ticket-taker yet. As the old sedan rounded the corner, Keeny ran to the curb with the dummy. The front door on the curb side flew open. He laid the dummy flat on the car top, slid inside, then reached out the window to keep the dummy from sailing off in the wind. On the other side of the car, Pelón and Shorty did the same.

They took off.

Twenty minutes later, Pelón parked in the alley behind the police station. Keeny crawled out. "Thanks, *amigos!*" He carried the dummy and his purchases across the empty parking lot, past the rusty gas pump, down the driveway, and pushed the side door open.

Upstairs, he placed the general on a table in the coffee room, where 'Miliano towered like a benevolent giant. His eyes looked down on Keeny, glossy-brown eyes gleaming with life. Keeny held his breath. Again he had that weird feeling that 'Miliano was going to speak!

"Hey, 'Miliano!" he said softly. "Hey, man!"

Zapata smiled, but could not be conned into speaking.

Chapter 11

With the general on watch outside his cell, Keeny slept better than he had in months. For comfort and tranquility, home could not touch it. In the morning, he moved 'Miliano back to the coffee room while he made himself some breakfast. Every time he looked at the dummy, he grinned with satisfaction.

He washed his utensils and put all his supplies away very neatly. Then he made his cot with as much care as though a Saturday inspection in prison were coming up. He felt sure the general would have insisted on a clean camp; and also, with all the disorder inside his head, he needed no clutter outside.

By ten o'clock, however, he had run out of things to do. He wished he had his schoolbooks. This, he realized, was like a man on Death Row wanting a calendar for Christmas. What good were schoolbooks to a kid who was going back to prison? Who at best might graduate with a trade like shoemaking?

But in his heart he was expecting 'Miliano to work a miracle for him—to trigger, somehow, an idea that would defeat the Rock and send Joaquín Durán back to the sidewalk, free. And not back to his nuthouse of a home, either, but to his own pad.

Where? How? That was where his ideas ran out.

Recalling the bale of newspapers in the basement, he carried a few of them up. They went clear back to the Fifties. Mice had eaten holes in them. As he read, he began to understand why they had been saved.

One paper headlined: U.S. PUTS 30-LB. SATELLITE IN ORBIT!

Another: CASTRO ASSUMES POWER IN CUBA! BATISTA FLEES!

FRENCH EXPLODE NUCLEAR DEVICE IN SAHARA! was another.

Someone had started a collection of memorable headlines. But evidently his collection had been outclassed as the bombs and the wars got bigger, so he had given up.

He read about flu outbreaks . . . the deaths of famous men . . . crimes . . . skirts getting shorter . . . skirts getting longer. . . .

One story intrigued him.

Somewhere in the South, an epidemic of sleeping sickness had swept a school. Most of the kids fell asleep at their desks and had to be carried out. The epidemic had been going on for a week when the story was written, and doctors thought it was caused by hysteria. Probably it would clear up eventually, they said. He guessed it must have, or he would have read about it.

After lunch he lay down for a nap. He slept soundly. As he was waking, he heard a footfall in the corridor.

Alarmed, he peered down the dingy hall. A dark figure stood gazing into the coffee room. His hair was black, his clothes were black; he was black from head to foot and looked like the Angel of Death. Keeny saw no gun in his hand. The figure leaned forward to squint into the coffee room.

"Hey, Keeny!" he called in a loud whisper.

Keeny groaned with relief. It was Little Apache, Apache's wayward younger brother.

"Yeah, man," he called.

"Where you at?"

"In the trusty cell."

Little Apache entered the cell and grinned down at him. He wore black bell-bottom trousers and a black tee shirt. His heavy, rich black hair was cut full, but trimmed carefully around the ears and in back. On his forearms were a variety of tattoos. His teeth shone in a broad smile. He giggled.

"Jeez, I thought that was you in the coffee room, with the gun!"

Keeny folded his arms behind his head. "Looks like me, huh?"

"Sure does. My brother told me how to get in, so I came."

"How come you're not in school?"

"Well, you know, what a drag! And I've got something going over in the Hole."

"I heard about it."

Little Apache bit his lower lip and giggled. Then he covered his mouth and laughed. "She's a real nice girl," he said. He tried to stop laughing, but was unable to. Little Apache was a funny dude. The more serious a thing was to him, the more he laughed about it. Once, just when he was about to be busted for assault, Keeny had seen him laugh so hard he collapsed on the floor.

"She may be nice," said Keeny, "but watch yourself, buddy. You can't trust any girl. She might be just setting the Aztecs up for the Cobras."

Little Apache ducked his head and continued giggling. "Oh, no, I trust her, man. She's great."

"Uh-huh," Keeny said. "How about a cup of coffee, *camarado?*"

Little Apache had to lean against the wall in his

laughter. "Yeah, that'd be good. Only, see—my girl, Yo-Yo—she's got a problem. . . ."

Keeny yawned and scrubbed his face with his palms. "That doesn't keep us from having a cup of coffee, does it?"

"I mean, like, she's *here,* man! She wants to talk to you."

Keeny lurched up in fury. "She's *here?*"

Little Apache put up both hands. "Hey, no, listen! She's all right! She won't tell anybody about you."

Keeny rammed him back against the bars. "You idiot! *You brought a girl here?*"

Little Apache giggled uncontrollably. "Man, she's a hundred percent! Wait till you meet her—"

Down the hall a girl's voice called. "Hey! Where are you?"

Keeny, his shoulders slumping, went to meet her.

In the coffee room, they found a small Mexican girl standing before the general. She wore a green blouse and skirt separated by six inches of skin. Green plastic boots were zipped to her knees. She carried a shopping bag of purple string which seemed to be filled with clothing and a big pink plastic mirror. She wore a single earring—a long gold chain with a star at the end of it. The amazing thing about her was her hair, lemon-yellow and standing out at least a foot around her head in an enormous bubble hairdo. It was like the mating plumage of some strange bird. And indeed she stood out, with her bizarre coloring and makeup, like a vivid parrot that had flown into a hen-yard from the jungle. In the middle of that fantastic hairdo was a very small, pretty face caked with makeup.

She smiled brazenly at Keeny. "Hi, cutie," she said.

"Did you know you could get busted for being in here?" Keeny retorted.

"So I get busted," Yo-Yo said. She dropped her shopping bag, lifted 'Miliano by the waist, and began dancing with him. Keeny tore her hands from the dummy and shoved her away.

"Hands off," he said. "Nobody touches him but me."

Yo-Yo smirked. "Oh, *excuse* me! I didn't know you two were sweethearts."

Keeny slapped her. Yo-Yo leaped at him like a cat. He slapped her again and pushed her down violently on one of the benches, then turned to Little Apache.

"Take charge of this broad before I throw her downstairs!" he said. "Man, we've sure got some rapping to do!"

He made coffee and had them sit across the table from him. Yo-Yo settled down. She took the mirror from her bag and examined her face.

"What'd you bring her here for?" Keeny asked.

"She's been living in a work-home," said Little Apache. "She got thrown out of school yesterday and the woman slapped her and said she was going to call her probation officer."

"People are always slapping me," said Yo-Yo, smiling at Keeny.

"I still don't dig why you brought her, man," Keeny said. "What am I supposed to do with her?"

"You're the guy with the ideas, Keeny. I thought maybe you could tell her what to do. She's not going back to the work-home."

Keeny spread his hands on the table top. He thought, sighed, shook his head.

"What's the dummy supposed to be?" asked Yo-Yo.

"That's 'Miliano Zapata," Keeny muttered.

Yo-Yo turned her head. "Hi, 'Miliano. What are *you* in for?"

"The point," Keeny said, "is what are you in for?"

"I need a place to stay."

"Well, this isn't it. I don't need a contributing charge."

"She's sorry about the dummy," said Little Apache. "She was just messing around."

"How come you don't live at home?" Keeny asked the girl.

"I can't get along with my stepfather," Yo-Yo said. Peering into the mirror, she stripped off the false eyelashes that had come loose, replaced the strip, then batted her lashes at Keeny and grinned.

Keeny glanced hopelessly at 'Miliano. His mind told him that his hideout was now useless; that he could not trust the girl to keep it secret. But his heart would not accept it.

What do I do now, man? he asked silently. *They've really put me down.*

The dummy seemed to reply with a small, secret smile. *No, hijo,* he might be saying. *Nobody can put you down unless you let him.*

Keeny thought about that. It was true. Nobody could sink you unless you panicked and let him. He felt cheered.

"What's the matter at home?" he asked. "Can't you go back there?"

"Everything's the matter," said Yo-Yo.

"Can't you stay there one night? See, I need time to think about this."

Little Apache put his arm across Yo-Yo's shoulders. "What about Engracia's place? You stayed there once, didn't you?"

"Yes, but her mother threw me out. I could stay with Lucha, I think."

"Take her to Lucha's," Keeny told Little Apache quickly. "I've got an idea that I'll work on tonight. I can't have her here, though, because the Man might walk in any time. Okay?"

Yo-Yo shrugged. "Okay."

Little Apache said seriously, "She's had a rough time, man. Her father died when she was little and her mother got killed by a man she was going with. She has these dreams—"

"Oh, shut up," Yo-Yo told him. She got up and stuffed the mirror into the shopping bag. From the door, she smiled brilliantly at Keeny, that fantastic yellow globe of hair standing out around her tiny face. "I won't tell anybody, Keeny. Don't worry."

"What's one more worry?" Keeny said.

"I really won't," the girl repeated. And he felt then, perhaps foolishly, that he could count on her not to betray him.

Chapter 12

Soon after dark, the Aztecs began arriving. Singly and in pairs, they came from the alley, slipping into the station house quickly and closing the door behind them. Pelón told Keeny that individual members were not being watched, so far as they knew; but certainly a cruising cop who recognized an Aztec would tail him for a couple of blocks. So they had parked on a side street, scattered, and come down the alley with the stealth of cats.

With them, they brought two half-gallon bottles of muscatel and a bag of tacos. Keeny was uneasy about the wine. Wine equaled good times; good times meant noise. How would the general have handled such a thing? He decided the general would have let them have their party but he himself would have stayed on top of things. So he ate and drank with them, but held himself back.

"I had company today," he said, looking pointedly at Apache. "Just like at honor camp."

"Oh, yeah?" said Apache.

"Yeah, man. Your brother brought his girl here."

Apache lowered a taco, a cigarette fuming in his hand. "When was this?" he asked.

"This afternoon."

The boys looked pained. They turned their eyes to Apache, who shook his head.

"I don't know about that cat, sometimes," he said.

Suddenly Pelón raised his hand. Pelón had the ears

of a cat. Now Keeny heard the noise, too: the rattling of a door. He felt a brief shock of fear, but he decided that the ones to worry about were those who had keys: the cops. This could be kids, a bum looking for a place to flop, anything. He signaled the others to sit tight and went out into the hall.

The rattling continued. It came from downstairs. In the sound there was a kind of weary desperation, like a hurt dog scratching at a door. Still holding a taco, he descended.

"Keeny!" a voice called.

Against the barred glass of the side door he saw a silhouette. After a moment he turned the latch. The door banged open. A boy dressed in black staggered inside and fell on the floor. It was Little Apache.

Keeny locked the door and called for help. Little Apache's face was terribly and unevenly swollen, as though it had been stung by hornets. One eye was completely closed, the other barely open. And his battered mouth was grotesquely swollen.

Pelón went out and came back with first-aid supplies. Little Apache lay on a table. He moaned and tried to sit up when Pelón poured Mercurochrome in a cut on his head. The gash was only about an inch long, but it went to the skull. Keeny could see a blue-white gleam of bone.

Mousie stood by, holding a roll of gauze. "Maybe you ought to take him to the hospital," he said.

"No. Not till we know what happened. The Man may be looking for him."

"Cobras!" Little Apache mumbled.

Apache bent over his brother. "What happened?"

"I took Yo-Yo home in your car. They were waiting for me."

"That damned Yo-Yo!" Apache said, straightening.

"No! She didn't know." Little Apache rolled his head.

"The hell she didn't! I *told* you—"

Keeny moved Apache aside. "Let's get this job done, man," he said. "Have some wine. And get him some."

Keeny had had his own injuries tended often enough, in jails and in clinics, to know that the main part of the treatment consisted in asking you to sign a complaint against the guys who had beaten you. Little Apache would live.

"Got any downers?" he asked Mousie.

Mousie took off his hat and began extracting red capsules from the inside of the sweatband. "How many you need?"

"He ought to have about three, and I could use one myself. And let's get that wine going, how 'bout it?"

Apache watched the wine going around and said in irritation: "Don't get too loaded. We're going down to the Hole when we get through and catch us a Cobra. Still got that starter's pistol?" he asked Goyo.

Goyo said he had. "But I ain't got any shells."

"We'll get shells."

"Where's the wine?" Keeny urged. "This guy's hurting."

They got the sleeping pills and a cup of wine into Little Apache. Keeny popped a capsule into his own mouth and drank from one of the bottles. He handed the bottle to Apache. While Apache drank, Keeny spat out the sleeping pill and hid it in his pocket. Mousie handed pills around. Getting loaded before a fight was an important part of the show, like an Indian wardance before a battle. The trick was to sharpen your courage without taking the edge off your anger.

Keeny brought a mattress from the cell and they laid Little Apache on it. He was limp.

"Did you get out with my car?" Apache asked him.

The wine and pills had slowed Little Apache almost to a stop. His lips moved for a while before any sound came out. "Down the street," he murmured.

Apache seemed relieved. He had a deep affection for the car, which he called The Oldest Pontiac in the World.

Keeny took another drink of muscatel and passed the jug to Apache. Pelón drank from the other bottle and gave it to Goyo. Deadpan, Pelón winked at Keeny. He knew the Aztecs were not a fighting gang; that Little Apache should not have been in the Cobras' beat. Pelón did not want to go on a disastrous raid any more than Keeny did.

Wine and pills were beginning to numb the Aztecs' brains. Everyone was running out of gas. They talked more slowly and did a lot of deep thinking before speaking. But Apache, who by now was as drunk as anyone, suddenly swayed to his feet.

"You guys go to hell! I'm going to burn me a Cobra."

"Okay, okay!" Pelón said. "But not tonight, man. They'll be waiting for us."

"Anybody going with me?" Apache asked. "Or are you all chicken? Get up, Goyo. You never chickened out of anything the longest day you lived."

Apache shook his shoulder until Goyo reluctantly got up. Apache said, "Come on— Mousie— Gato— *Vámonos!*"

Keeny watched the boys get up. "What are you going to do?" he challenged Apache. "Go charging in and let them corner you in a dead-end street? You don't righteously know the country. It's a jungle down there, dirt streets, mud, no real streets at all."

"I don't have to know it," Apache retorted. "We aren't getting out of the car unless we have to. We're going to get Goyo's *cuete* and look for Cobras on the street."

Keeny watched the others get up, one by one, dazed, with drugs but sparked to life by Apache's appeal. He glanced at 'Miliano. *What next?* he asked silently. *What do I do?*

The general seemed to observe the scene with disapproval; his thin, dark face was somber. His arm upraised, he seemed to warn:

Stop, batos! Are you crazy? You'll never get out of there alive.

Keeny heard the noise of the Aztecs' departure suddenly cease. All of the boys turned to stare, astounded, at General Zapata.

"Hey man!" Apache croaked. "Who said that?"

Slowly Keeny got up. Though he did not understand it, there was a weird, gooseflesh-y feeling in him that something very odd was taking place.

"Nobody said anything, man," he said. "Like what?"

"Like not getting out alive. *Somebody* said that. It didn't sound like you, man."

The boys came back into the room, to stand puzzled before the general. Keeny lowered himself onto a bench, trembling.

Now, this is very weird! he told himself, trying to understand it. *These dudes read my mind some way! But six guys can't read your mind all at once. So what's going on?*

"Man, you *musta* said it!" Pelón said. "Because I heard it loud and clear. There's nobody else here."

Keeny said: "I might've *thought*—what you said—but I didn't say anything."

"Then who said it?"

I, 'Miliano, said the same voice.

The boys looked at Keeny, at each other, and began moving away from the cardboard general.

Chapter 13

Keeny felt them all staring at him. It was somehow up to him to make sense of it. "Excuse me, General," he said, "but my name is Durán, not Zapata."

But your parents come from Morelos, where I lived.

"I—I think so."

Your great-grandmother was of my bloodline, the general said.

Keeny frowned at his hands. "Excuse me," he said, "but dummies—I mean cardboard—can't talk."

Of course not. I speak with my heart but your tongue.

"Like a ventriloquist's dummy?" Apache said. "I've seen that on TV."

"That's all it is!" said Goyo, suddenly relieved. "He's throwing his voice."

They all began to laugh, even the general. As they laughed, Keeny put his fingers to his throat. He felt the vibrations of the general's laughter. He felt relieved, yet let down. So that was all it was. They were loaded, and that had made it easy to believe that the general was really talking. But it had really been himself, voicing the things he was thinking.

Now the other boys began to chatter, as they gained confidence. "That's all it was!" one said. "He was throwing his voice."

"Just like a ventriloquist!"

Pelón poked Keeny. "Man, for a minute there I thought I was losing my mind."

They laughed, keeping the laughter going long after they thought it was funny. When they quieted down, Keeny said:

"Yeah, that's got to be it. But you know something, *batos*? I never knew Zapata lived in Morelos! So how come I said it?"

"Maybe he didn't," said Apache. "You saying it don't make it so."

"That's right," Goyo agreed.

The general startled them all by saying: *Look it up.*

They gaped at him. It seemed to Keeny that the general stared back at them, haughtily. Finally he said:

Look up March 11, 1911, while you're doing it. Laugh about that one, batos! Look up my Plan de Ayala, too: "Land for the Indians!" And look it up about my name, "written in gold!"

Keeny felt them pitting themselves against the miracle. Only he was full of the will to believe. He knew that even if it was his voice speaking, it was not his mind dictating the words, for he knew nothing of these things the general spoke about.

He was the ventriloquist's dummy, not 'Miliano.

"It's a snow job," said Apache. "I can recognize your voice, now that I know it's you."

"Nobody said it wasn't. But it's not me saying that stuff, because I never heard it before. Look it up, like he says. Maybe you'd better look at the dummy, too, and see if I taped a speaker onto the back of it."

They turned the dummy around and searched. There was nothing there. The general was silent. Abashed, they put questions to him afterward, but he

84

did not speak again. He was only a cardboard cutout with no special powers at all.

"Show's over," Keeny said, suddenly tired. "You guys had better get Little Apache home."

Lying on his bunk later, he thought wearily, *That was really a high. A high like that I don't need. I wonder who put acid in the wine?*

In the morning, he was reluctant to enter the coffee room. Finally he went in, but kept his eyes off 'Miliano as he prepared breakfast. He opened a can of fruit juice and a box of cereal. He heated coffee water and set out eggs and bread. He had got in the habit of eating a big breakfast in prison. He put the eggs to boil in the coffee water and sat down with his fruit juice and cereal. As he was finishing the cereal, he shot a furtive look at the dummy.

Zapata seemed to be smiling. Despite himself, Keeny grinned. Then the general laughed, a boisterous laugh, and Keeny found himself laughing too. Finally the general said:

Are you afraid of me, Joaquín?

"No, man. But nothing like this ever happened to me before. I'm talking to myself!"

Don't worry. Most people do it.

"But they don't answer themselves!"

He caught himself almost offering the general some coffee. He bent his head over his plate and set to eating industriously. He made toast over the hot plate and lathered it with jelly. But not for a second could he forget 'Miliano. It was like eating with the President of the United States sitting there watching you.

Finished eating, he looked at the dummy again.

"How'm I going to get out of this box, hombre?" he asked.

You shouldn't have gone into it. It's their box, not yours. You should have gone with the police that night and let your P.O. help you.

"But I didn't. So what can I do now?"

I don't know. Why don't you let your parole officer help you?

"Mr. Baker? What can he do? The cops don't like P.O.'s anyway, and with a warrant out for me his hands are tied."

What you're saying is that it's impossible to get out of the mess you're in, then?

Keeny rested his head in his hands, elbows planted on the table. "Yeah."

Well, if that's it, said 'Miliano, *why not turn yourself in and start doing your time?*

"Because I'm not ready to quit. I really feel like— like I'm as smart as the Rock is, and if I—hell, I don't know what I mean," he finished.

"—Keeny?" a girl's voice said behind him. "Hey, can I come in?"

He remembered, then, going to bed so groggy last night that he had forgotten to lock the door. And now here was this girl, Yo-Yo, moving in on him again! He turned on the bench to face the small, disheveled girl in the wrinkled green two-piece dress who stood in the doorway, her string shopping bag hanging from her hand.

"You're in, aren'cha?" he said.

Yo-Yo smiled and drifted inside. "Hi!" She looked around, puzzled. That fabulous yellow hair of hers, a tangled bubble, dwarfed the little face in the center of it. She looked like a slovenly doll.

"Who were you talking to?" she asked. "I thought some of the other guys were here."

"I was talking to 'Miliano."

"But I heard another guy talking to you—"

"That was 'Miliano. Say hello to Yo-Yo, 'Miliano."

Yo-Yo started as the general's voice boomed out heartily. *Hello, chamaca!* he said. *Make yourself at home.*

Yo-Yo stared at the dummy. She grinned distrustfully at Keeny. "What's going on? How do you do that?"

He *doesn't do it,* said 'Miliano. *I do it. Sit down. Can I offer you some coffee?*

Yo-Yo giggled and sat down near Keeny. "Sure. Hey, that's too much!" she told Keeny. "Is there a microphone?"

Keeny put his hand on her shoulder. "What there is," he said, "is something pretty weird. If you don't like weird stuff, maybe you'd better split. The dummy started talking last night."

He walked to the sink and plugged in the hot plate.

Don't send her away, said Zapata. *I want to talk to this girl. I want to know whether she finked on Little Apache.*

Keeny glanced around, and Yo-Yo was melting down on the bench like putty. She was white as a candle. Her thin shoulders slumped. Her shopping bag toppled over on the floor.

"What is this?" she whispered.

"I told you!" Keeny said. "Don't ask me. He used my mouth, if you want the truth, but he knows things I don't. Maybe you'd *better* take off, because I've got a feeling he's going to get on your case, and you may not like what he says about you."

Yo-Yo covered her face. "I didn't do it!" she wept. "'Miliano, I didn't know they were going to do it! I was at Lucha's all night."

Keeny smiled at her. Girls were too much! While the Aztecs were doing research to decide whether the general was a fraud, Yo-Yo had already bought him.

Women *wanted* to believe stuff like this. His mother had visions of things that were going to happen—and often they did. His grandmother had awakened one night and cried, "Papa's dead!" And five hundred miles away, they learned later, his grandfather had died that night.

Yo-Yo already believed in 'Miliano more than Keeny did.

If you didn't fink on Little Apache, said the general, *how did you know the Cobras had jumped him?*

"A friend of Lucha's called her this morning and told her. The girl goes with one of the Cobras."

Keeny swished the coffee water around in the pan. "They messed him up good," he said. "'Miliano had to talk the Aztecs out of going down to the Hole and burning a Cobra. I'm telling you straight, Yo-Yo, if they find you here they'll probably cut off your hair. Or worse."

Someone should, said the general.

Shyly, Yo-Yo made passes at her hair. Then she groped in her bag. "I haven't brushed it yet this morning," she said.

'Miliano snorted. *Brushing won't help. A chicana should have black or brown hair, to go with her eyes and skin. And your skin! Why is it so yellow, like a lemon?*

"I—I use a light powder base."

Powder base? Yellow hair? I don't know about those things. All I know is that in Morelos women were proud of their hair and skin. They used brushes on their hair, and soap and water on their skin. Women did not look like freaks, in my day.

Yo-Yo hung her head. Feeling sorry for her, Keeny said:

"You're kind of cutting her down, General. I really do think she's okay. She's got this lousy deal where she has no righteous home, you see? Her mother can't tell her how to dress and stuff, because she's dead. And she has these bad dreams and all—"

Her hair would give me bad dreams, said the general.

Yo-Yo began to cry. Keeny sat beside her and put his arm around her shoulders. She put her face against his chest and wailed. In her ear, he whispered:

"Why don't you get some junk and dye your hair back to its natural color? The roots are already black. And maybe you can kind of braid it or—you know."

And what is this about having no mother? 'Miliano went on, relentlessly. *Isn't there a stepmother?*

Yo-Yo's head turned. "I hate her! Because she hates me. I'd rather stay in the work-home."

What is the work-home?

"The Rehab woman put me there. The place was all right at first, but now they use me like a slave. Mrs. Nava makes me do the dishes and iron clothes."

Well, why not? Don't she and her husband give you your clothes and your board? And a little money?

"Yes, but—"

Does she let you go to school?

"Yes, only I got thrown out because—well, the girls' vice-principal hates me."

Why?

Keeny listened to them talk, not trying to understand how the process worked. You did not have to know how a radio operated in order to listen to it.

"Well, see, she told me to wear longer dresses. And my clothes are my own business. It's a new school to me, too. It was all right at first. I had a big sister to show me around, but the teachers are all down on me because I lived in the Hole and now I live in El Sereno. All middle-class Mexicans—*Tío Tacos.*"

She hesitated, seeming to realize, as she heard her

arguments, that much of what she said was nonsense. 'Miliano said, *Go on. I'm listening.*

Yo-Yo talked on, stopping now and then to blow her nose. The tests showed that she wasn't dumb, she said, but the teachers hated her for some reason. Most of the kids hated her too. Mrs. Nava hated her. So she made her iron clothes and wash dishes and be in by ten o'clock.

You said things were all right "at first," commented 'Miliano. *Everything seems to go all right for you "at first," then it blows up. Even though you had to do chores "at first," and bring your homework to class, it was all right. What happens to spoil things?*

"I don't know. I guess I get sick of it," said Yo-Yo.

I got sick of being the lowest-paid private in the Mexican cavalry, too, said 'Miliano. *I had great dreams, though, and I read books and made plans. I wanted land for all the peasants. When it was time, I raised an army and captured southern Mexico from the Federales. But I didn't do it by dying my hair yellow and staying out all night. I worked, chamaca. I struggled!*

Yo-Yo looked up, tears streaming down her face. "'Miliano," she pleaded, *"who are you?"*

Keeny was sure the general smiled. *I am Emiliano Zapata,* he said. *Who are you? A chicana? A rebel? A fool? Or what?*

"I don't know," Yo-Yo said miserably.

What is your real name?

"María de la Concepción."

Then we'll call you Concha. That's at least a start.

Chapter 14

Concha hurried from the station in the light rain that had begun to fall, and when she returned she carried several parcels. She sang Mexican love songs as she worked around the coffee room. She asked Keeny's permission to set 'Miliano up on a table in a corner. He agreed.

In a murky water glass, she put some geraniums she had stolen from someone's garden. She arranged them on the table before the dummy.

"Hey, slow down!" Keeny told her, beginning to be bothered. "Don't get carried away. I don't even know what the guys will find out about him. If that stuff he said didn't make sense, he's still just a dummy."

Concha put her hands on her hips. "I don't think you have any right to talk like that in front of him."

From another parcel the girl took a red cotton dress with white trim. She hung it in the closet. Then she placed on the sink some bottles and a plastic bowl.

"What's all that?" he asked her.

"Hair tint. I'm going to dye my hair black again." Looking at Keeny with a quiet smile, she smoothed her hair back from her forehead. "I may decide to be a nun," she said.

"Uh-huh," Keeny said. "But maybe you ought to get off probation, first. Where'd you steal the dress?"

"I didn't steal it. It was only four dollars. All I stole is the hair dye, and I'll pay them back some day."

Concha had brought some schoolbooks in her shopping bag. She got them out.

"Do you want to read any of these? There's some short stories in the Language book."

Keeny went to his cell and read, while Concha started the hair-dyeing process, which seemed to be something like a Black Mass, full of mystery and ritual. He read until he was sleepy, then napped. When he awoke, he shuffled back to the coffee room to scare up some lunch. But Concha was already heating beans and wieners on the hot plate, her head wrapped in a towel. Not a hair showed. She wore the red dress and had toned down her eye makeup until she no longer looked like some rare bird.

After lunch, she went over and sat on a bench before 'Miliano. Suddenly, before Keeny knew what was happening, she had slipped to the floor and was kneeling before him! He grimaced. Yesterday she was the worst chick in Dogtown, or runner-up; today she was trying to be the best.

" 'Miliano," he heard her murmur, *"te adoro!"*

Keeny walked over and sat down near her. "Listen, baby, you've got to cut this out!" he reasoned. "He isn't God, he's cardboard. I stole him from a theater. And whatever he is, you can't—you know—worship him."

With her turbaned head bowed, Concha said in a soft, churchy voice: "You can't understand because you aren't a girl, Keeny."

"He uses my mouth to talk to you, doesn't he? So I guess I'm in on the deal."

"He doesn't use your mind. His spirit fills this room, Keeny! It's a miracle! *Un milagro!*"

Keeny rested his chin in his cupped hand, his elbow balanced on one knee. "You make me feel like a Plaza preacher, *mujer.*"

Looking up at 'Miliano, Concha asked in a soft voice: "What do you want me to do, 'Miliano?"

'Miliano said: *What do you want to do, girl?*

"I want to be good. I don't want to fight with everyone always. I just want to believe everybody, and like them. I don't want to live out of a shopping bag, and I'd like to have my own room and keep it clean, and my clothes hung up, and study. I could finish school and be a nun—or a nurse—"

Go back to the work-home. Tell the Navas you're sorry. Show the children you love them.

"Oh, I will!"

It won't be easy, Concha, warned the general. *But when it's hard, close your eyes and listen—*

Concha bit her lip. "Only . . . the bad dreams I have, 'Miliano. They scare me so much! Sometimes I do bad things because I don't want to think about them. The dreams are . . . like snakes in a pit—all tangled—and I've got to untangle them. . . ."

'Miliano said gently: *The dreams were the hate you felt. You won't have them anymore.*

"May I stay here tonight?" asked the girl. "I want to think, and to—to fix my hair—"

You may stay tonight.

Keeny felt a flash of irritation. The pad was his, not 'Miliano's! The risk of her being here was his, too.

"Wait a minute!" he said. "If the Man finds her here it'll be on my record that I contributed to the delinquency of a minor."

'Miliano did not reply. Neither he nor the girl seemed to regard his presence as important.

"I am ashamed," Concha said, "that I stole the stuff for my hair, 'Miliano."

*You should be. It was a small store. The people who
own it work hard for their money. Leave the money
on the counter, but don't say anything to them.*

"I would have paid, only I ran out of money."

Keeny will give it to you.

Keeny bounced up, stared at Concha's rapturous,
uplifted face, and dug down in his pocket. He pulled
out a dollar and dropped it on the floor by her.
"You're welcome!" Then he kicked her shopping bag
and went to his cell. She was taking 'Miliano away
from him! Making him into some kind of plaster saint.
The Miracle of Chicago Street Police Department!
That was not the idea at all! 'Miliano was a revolutionary. Women, in his life, were *soldaderas* who trav-
eled with his army and cooked for his soldiers, and
slept with them, too.

Lying on his rack, he thought, *Man, whose dummy
are you? Who brought you to life? Who are you if I
walk out of here?*

He saw that he had 'Miliano in his fist.

And yet. . . . When he faced him, he was trapped
in a kind of trance, like Concha. In some mysterious
way, 'Miliano was something different to everyone.
He was God to Concha, a father and a fighter to
Keeny, a cheap trick to Apache.

What was he really?

After dark, Keeny went downstairs and unlocked the
door. The Aztecs arrived a few minutes after he went
back upstairs. He heard them tramping in like storm
troopers.

"Hide in the closet!" he told Concha. "They've still
got it in their heads that you finked on Little Apache."

As the door closed on the girl, Pelón, Apache, Goyo,
and Gato entered the coffee room. In a glance Keeny
saw that all were loaded, and that Gato was strung

out. His nose was running and he was scratching himself. Gato got right down to personal problems, while the others went over to the dummy and stared at it.

"Goldie got busted!" he whined to Keeny. "He was my connection. Ask the dummy where I can get a couple of *gramos*."

Pelón, wearing a black sweatshirt, pushed the sleeves up to his elbows and glared about the room. "Shut up, Gato," he snarled. "Has that tramp, that Yo-Yo, been back?" he asked.

"No, man," Keeny said. "What's happening?"

Apache said, "We got shot up at a drive-in! Two bullets through my windshield, and a tire shot out."

"The Cobras?"

"Yeah. I seen Ruco driving. Yo-Yo must have phoned them that we were at the Submarine Base."

"Maybe. Maybe not. Were you already loaded then?"

"We're not loaded now," said Pelón, his eyes dull. "We've only dropped a few." He pulled from his pocket a small, nickeled pistol, almost a toy. "*Mire!*" he said.

What is it with Aztecs? said the general, contemptuously. *You can't defend yourselves in your own country, but you want to go raiding into theirs!*

"How much do we have to take before it's right to square with them?" Keeny asked.

Turn it over to the police, the general argued.

"The Rock would look the car over and give Apache a ticket for defective tires. That's the kind of police protection *we* get."

Gato was tugging at his sleeve. "Ask him—!" he urged. "Where can I get a *gramo*? I've got to get fixed, man!"

"I told you if you kept geezing, you'd get burned.

95

I'll go with you guys," he said to the others. "Is it still raining?"

"A little," Pelón said.

Keeny walked to the general and confronted him. "What do you say, man? This is your kind of raid. How would you run it?"

He was not sure what he was expecting, but what he got was silence. He felt a sharp sense of disappointment. He had long since had it with saints and prayers. But for a while he had felt as though he had been given something again. A father who would love and guide him and not die, as his own father had.

As the boys went crowding out of the room, Keeny caught Pelón's arm. "Pelón. Man," he said. "Did you look it up? About 'Miliano?"

Pelón frowned. "Yeah. . . ."

"Well, what—?"

". . . March 11, 1911, was when he began his rebellion against the *Federales*. I guess you'd read it somewhere—"

"Uh-huh," Keeny said, deadpan. "And what about his name—'written in gold'?"

"It's written in gold in the Chamber of Deputies, in Mexico City. . . ."

Keeny, following him from the room, knew he had never read anything about 'Miliano Zapata. He knew little more about him than the general himself had told him. The miracle was not so simple as his merely throwing his voice. For in some way, the general had also taken charge of his mind.

Chapter 15

You could drive from Happy Valley to the Hole in ten minutes; but it was like crossing the border into some hostile country where you entered by night with a trench knife, emergency rations, and a compass. As bad as Happy Valley was, the Hole was worse. In its mile-square triangle, hardly a streetlight broke the dark clusters of mean little houses and trees. The few lights were broken as fast as they were replaced.

By day, the black and brown slum had a disheveled charm, its dirt lanes rambling without plan like the footprints of a dog chasing shorebirds on a beach. Smogblighted orange and eucalyptus trees, the remnants of old groves, stood like scarecrows among the houses. Many of the dwellings were homemade, nailed together from signs and packing boxes and resting on little heaps of boulders or concrete blocks.

In the winter, mud puddles glistened like small lakes in the streets. In some of the houses there would be electric lights; but more often the glow against the ragged curtains was thrown by coal-oil lamps. Keeny had been through the Hole a couple of times on a dare. He knew that on the south it was bounded by a fenced-off freeway and a steep, grassy rise where kids dug caves. At the top of the rise a housing project stood like a pink fortress. To the north was the concrete-lined bank of the Angelus River.

In the dark lanes and alleys of the Hole roved a subculture of gangs interrelated like the Mafia. Some, like the Cobras, had been swinging for fifty years. The grandchildren of the original gangs ran with the Hole gangs now. Every kid on the street belonged to some gang or other. You were either a member of a gang or you did not live in the Hole. Not for long.

Apache, driving The Oldest Pontiac in the World with five Aztecs crowded into it, slowed down at the top of the bluff above the Hole. Keeny could see the lights of Old River Road, the area's main street, running down to a dead end at the riverbed.

"Better stop a minute," he said.

Apache parked. Pelón took a drink from a bottle of wine and passed it to Keeny. Keeny said:

"No, man. I'm waiting till we get back. What'd you guys have in mind, now?"

It turned out that what they had in mind was that he should mastermind the raid. Pelón put it to him.

"What do you say? We've got to hit and run, I figure, because I get it that these dudes have a telephone watch. When anybody comes in that they don't know, the word goes out and the cats begin to move."

"It sounds to me like a bad scene, *batos*," Keeny said. He saw Pelón's face harden.

"Open the door," Pelón said. "Keeny wants out."

"No, man," Keeny said. "It's not going to be easy, though, and I'm just saying—it ain't my idea. I'll go along, but I'm not making book on getting out again."

Their silence was hostile. Here they were with a windshield cobwebbed by two Cobra bullets, a tire ruined by another, and he was talking peace.

"Okay," he said. "We look for a guy on watch. How do they work that?"

"What I hear, Ruco hangs out at a bar where there's a telephone, and they phone him there. Once they blockade Old River Road, there's no getting out without machine guns and rockets."

Keeny thought, *Then why are we going in?* He frowned at the dark flats below, dotted with yellow houselights and the glow of the main street. "You still figure to burn somebody, eh?"

"What else?" Apache retorted, rocking his foot on the accelerator. "They beat up my brother and shot up my car. We didn't come to yell swear-words at them."

"If we burn anybody, man," Keeny pointed out, "you'll have cops and Cobras on your necks for the rest of your natural lives."

Apache looked at him. "If you want to get out, man, now's a good time."

"All I want is to get out of the Hole alive. How about shooting him in the leg? Or what about if we pick him up and take him with us? Beat on him a while before we dump him out? If we get the telephone man, Ruco won't have the word before we finish up and take off."

There was a meditative silence.

"Yeah, man. That's good," Goyo said. Goyo was *muy hombre* and no one would down him, so Keeny relaxed.

"If the car conks out or anything like that," he said, "head for the river. You can slide down the concrete bank to the bottom and hike up to those steps under the Chicago Street Bridge."

"*Claro,*" said Pelón.

Apache argued for sniping at a man, but opinion had hardened against him. He laid the gun on the seat where he could get at it quickly. The engine bogged as Apache fed it some gas. It stuttered, then roared. They rolled down the street toward the river.

Unpaved lanes branched off to the right and left. They began to pass darkened stores, bar entrances as inviting as cavities in rotten teeth, and vacant lots lush with green weeds. Across from the A-1 Auto Wrecking was DR. H. J. SAENZ, PHYS. AND SUR.

Keeny forced his clenched fists open. It was not, he told himself, the Cobras he feared, but their reputation. In Deuell he had dreaded a bull of a boy who ran the *chicano* clique, knowing he *had* to fight him or be his slave. And when he fought him, Keeny was so much faster than this aborigine of a boy that it was like a butcherbird fighting an eagle.

"What's that there?" Pelón said, peering across an intersection.

On the right was a corner taco stand, a mere sheet-metal box with greasy windows. Near it stood a group of teen-agers. Above the stand was a picture of a spitting cat and the legend THE ALLEY CAT.

"Wait, wait!" Keeny gripped Apache's arm so suddenly that he braked short of the corner. "There's a phone booth!" he said. "Guy in it, too."

They peered at the unlighted booth at the far end of the paper-littered lot. Barely visible, a boy lounged in the old wooden booth, eating a taco in a waxed paper.

Nervously, Keeny wiped his mouth. "Me and Pelón'll haul him to the car," he said. "Goyo, have the back door open. We throw him in with you and Gato. We go on to the next block and turn right. Turn right again and come back this way a couple of blocks, then right again to Old River Road and back the way we came."

"What about the dude?"

"Beat on him as we go and we pitch him out somewhere—park near the booth after Pelón and I get out. Pelón?"

"Yeah, man!"

"Let's go!"

Keeny opened the door and sauntered to the screened window of the taco stand. He heard Pelón following him. The Hole kids standing around stared at him curiously.

"Give us five beef tacos, dad," he told the middle-aged man in a chili-stained white cap inside the stand.

"Coming up," the man said. "What to drink?"

"Nothing."

Keeny looked at Pelón, who was nervously raking his mustache with his long comb, looking strung out and pale. "Man," said Keeny, loudly, "I'd better call Tomás before we eat, or I'll forget." He started toward the booth.

"Phone's being used," said one of the boys standing nearby. He was short, strong, and well-proportioned, a miniature Hercules.

"We'll wait," Keeny said, reaching in his pocket as if for change as he walked. The car had coasted on and was waiting at the curb now, headlights dimmed. He heard the boy following him.

"I'll take this dude," he told Pelón. "Rip the phone wire loose and bust the other cat."

A few feet from the telephone booth he turned and spoke to the boy who was following them.

"Got a couple of dimes, *comarado?*"

The boy frowned, but, more or less automatically, with the inborn courtesy of the *chicano*, reached in his pocket. Keeny swung and caught him on the nose. It was the best place for a first shot, he always said, because it usually ended the fight. He saw blood spurt as he drove in and gave the Cobra a knee in the crotch. Moaning and bleeding, the boy dropped onto all fours.

Someone yelled: *"Al alba!"* It was the boy in the

telephone booth. Turning, Keeny saw Pelón rip the telephone from the Cobra's hand, yank the wire loose, then slug him with the instrument. But Keeny knew the word had gone out. There might still be time to get out, if they did not fool around—if the car did not break down—if—

Pelón hit the boy again and he staggered out, trying to swing, blood pouring from two cuts in his forehead. Pelón seized him by an arm and dragged him toward the car. Keeny caught his other arm and they half-dragged, half-pushed him toward the car. The kids on the corner had scattered, the girls screaming, more in delight than in fear. Pelón and Keeny hurled the Cobra into the back seat and slammed the door. They crowded into the front seat as Apache gunned the old engine.

At the next corner, Keeny braced himself for the turn. He heard grunts and groans in the back seat as Gato and Goyo pummeled the captured Cobra. The car rolled on blindly through the intersection, and Keeny turned on Apache.

"What are you doing?" he yelled. "I told you to turn right!" Apache stomped on the brake pedal, but the brakes were poor and the car kept rolling. "Keep going!" Keeny told him. "Turn at the next corner."

Loaded! Bombed! he thought bitterly. *Going out on a raid loaded!*

I told you, 'Miliano said. *I told you twice, but who can reason with a fool?*

"Shut up!" Keeny shouted at his fear.

The car smoked past a broken line of stores whose dark fronts were protected by metal grilles. At the next corner, Apache cramped the wheel and the car heeled into the turn like a battleship, slowly, ponderously. With the turn uncompleted, the left front wheel plowed into a curb and a tire blew with a whistling bang.

Cursing, Apache shoved the gearshift into reverse. They backed a few feet and he shifted again and they limped off down the street. The headlights illuminated the ground ahead. Potholes glistened with muddy water. On both sides were lines of trees and shacks, cars parked in front yards.

Headlights behind them lit up the interior of the old Pontiac. Pelón looked back and gasped, "Somebody tailing us!"

"Give it everything!" Keeny yelled.

Chapter 16

He had forgotten, if he had ever really known, what a jungle the Hole was, how a main cross-street might look like a driveway, so that only a resident could know whether it was a street or not. The old sedan splashed through deep puddles and slid along muddy ruts. The car behind tailgated them remorselessly, its lights scorching the rear window.

There was a flash. Keeny heard the report of a pistol shot as a bullet shattered the rear window. He hit Apache's arm and pointed.

"There's an alley ahead! Turn left, toward the river. We'll never get the car out. They'll have the street blocked by now. It's the only way. Where's your gun?"

"On the floor, I think—"

Keeny groped until he found the starter's pistol. Another shot ripped through the metal top of the sedan. He thrust his arm out the window and fired back at the car behind them, wondering, as he did so, if by some enormous stroke of bad luck it might be a police car. He heard the bullet scream off metal.

The other car fell behind.

Apache wrestled the sedan into what was either an alley or else a lane that lost itself in patches of dying orange trees. The wheels sank into mud. The blown front tire dropped a foot as the engine labored. The car slowed and stopped, its wheels spinning.

They abandoned the sedan and ran down the muddy lane. Keeny hurled the useless single-shot pistol into the orange trees. The mud sucked at his feet. He saw Pelón trip and go to his knees, and stopped to help him up.

"Bad scene!" Pelón panted.

"Keep moving, man. They're coming!"

The glare of headlights lit the scene with chalky brilliance. The old orange grove resembled a forest where a battle had been fought, that was lighted now by a flare. The Aztecs avoided the lighted ground beside the lane and held to the shadows flung down the middle of the ruts by the Pontiac. Keeny heard the other car halt behind the sedan with a clang of bumpers.

"Keep moving, keep moving!" he shouted.

Gasping, they slogged past a small shack with newspapers taped over the windows. Just beyond it, the lane swung right. The boys blindly started out in this new direction, but Keeny shouted at them to keep moving in the direction of the river, across lots.

Behind them two pistol shots cracked. Something snapped through the arthritic branches of a leafless orange tree near the road. The sound of Gato moaning came to him. Gato was falling behind. Keeny dropped back and got an arm around his waist to help him. Gato was almost past helping. He was doubled over with withdrawal cramps and sobbing in agony. To his physical distress was now added the poison of terror.

Pelón ran back and each boy brought one of Gato's arms around his neck. They hurried him forward with his toes dragging. *If* they *could make it to the riverbed,* Keeny thought, *the Cobras might not find him.*

Suddenly the old orange grove dropped into blackness. They were at the top of the long, concrete bank

of the river. It slid steeply to its half-mile-wide concrete bed. Keeny heard the other Aztecs already slipping and sliding down the long cement bank. He and
Pelón sat Gato on his rump and started him down the
embankment. Then they left him. It was every man
for himself.

Four of the boys reached the iron steps beneath the
bridge a half-hour later. Rain fell in a cold drizzle.
They rested at the foot of the stairs, panting, wiping
their noses, staring at one another with the dull eyes
of cattle. They had lost a man, a pistol, and an automobile; and they knew they were lucky.

"One man better go up every couple of minutes,"
Keeny said. "And stay off Chicago Street."

Apache said dazedly, "I guess 'Miliano called the
shot, huh?"

Pelón wagged his head bitterly and started up the
steps.

"How do you figure that March the Eleventh deal?"
Apache asked.

"I don't," Keeny said. "I don't figure any of it."

"Well, he was right. He was right."

They asked Keeny other questions about the dummy.

Did he talk all the time, like anybody else? Could
he predict the future? Keeny silently shook his head.
He did not want to talk about it until he began to
understand it. Maybe it was a miracle, as Concha
had said. Probably the less he said, he decided, the
better.

Somehow he was surprised to find the avenue looking
the same when he reached it—as though so much had
been changed for him, the street should seem changed,

too. He caught a bus and dropped off across from the Texaco station. Cars hurried by on the wet pavement. He trotted across on the green light and entered the telephone booth, leaving the door open so that the light would not come on. He did not like to get Mr. Baker out of bed, but he had the feeling that time was closing in on him.

"This is Keeny," he said.

"I thought it might be. I'd heard a rumor that you were alive and well and living in South America. But then I had a call from Sergeant Rock about a half-hour ago, and I wondered whether you weren't still in town."

"What did he call about?"

"A railroad detective picked Gato up in the river-bed tonight. He's strung out and babbling. He hadn't told them anything when Sergeant Rock called me, but the sergeant sounded pretty confident that he would. He just wanted me to know. What's happening, Keeny?" asked the parole officer.

"It's a long story. I'd like to talk to you tomorrow night, if I can."

"Why haven't you called me before?"

"Some pretty weird stuff has been going on, Mr. Baker. I don't dig it. Can I meet you someplace?"

"How about that parolee house I mentioned? I have a meeting planned with the boys. We can talk there. Of course, things have gone so far now that I don't know what I can tell you but to turn yourself in. Maybe I'd better just drive you over to Juvenile Hall and make sure you get a lawyer."

"No, man. With my luck, the kind of lawyer I'd draw would have seven fingers on each hand and half a deck upstairs. Where is the pad?"

Mr. Baker explained how to find the house. It was

in Happy Valley, only a couple of miles from Keeny's home. Come about seven, he said. . . . The landlady would give him some dinner.

Keeny stood a long time in the shadow of a telephone pole before stealing to the door of the police station. It was still unlocked. But when he went inside, the dim hallway vibrated with menace. He could taste danger on his tongue like sulfur fumes. Then he caught on, and identified the smell. *Cigar smoke!*

He stood in the main hallway for a full minute, listening. Not a sound but traffic broke the humming stillness. He went upstairs step by step. In his mind he saw the Rock waiting in the coffee room, sitting at a galvanized-iron table with a cigar in his mouth and a revolver on the table, grinning.

But he was not there.

Neither, for that matter, was 'Miliano.

Finally, in the closet, Keeny found the dummy with a note fixed to his hat by a hairpin. *"Dear Keeny: A wochmen came. Miliano and I hide in the closset until he wen away. He did not know nothing about us. And I put all your stuf out of site. Listen to Miliano, he is your frien. Concha."*

Keeny wearily carried the general back to his table and propped him upright. 'Miliano looked like a wise, forgiving father. Keeny gave him a tired hand-salute.

"Good night, General," he said. "It's been a bummer. You were right."

Chapter 17

The next night, wearing the red poncho and the narrow-brimmed black hat, Keeny stood on a corner in the windy darkness, scrutinizing a very large old house in Happy Valley at the address Mr. Baker had given him. The building had the towering, ornate lines of a steamboat, with a lot of intricate scrollwork decorating the eaves, a fanlight visible above the door, and even some stained glass glowing in the windows under a lofty gable.

A streetlamp threw the shadows of leggy shrubs against a long porch. Shadowy figures in porch chairs were silhouetted against the downstairs windows. A television set cast a blue glow on the front windows.

Well, go on in! he told himself.

But he did not know these kids, was not even sure he wanted to know them. It was like the first day in the joint, everybody trying to fit you into your slot, while you tried to fit them into theirs. He tossed the Mexican coin, pocketed it, and went up the walk. The boys ranged along the wall silently looked him over. He could not see their faces because of the light behind them.

"I'm looking for Mr. Baker," he said to the darkness.

A big, solidly built boy who wore long chestnut hair in a Prince Valiant cut said: "You're Joaquín, right?"

"Yeah—Durán."

"Hi, I'm Andy."

"Is he here?"

"Sure, go on in."

Keeny pulled the screen door open and went into a big, dim front room. Around the walls were ranged a number of old, deep chairs and two battered sofas. In these seats lounged a number of boys and two or three girls. At first glance the scene was not so different from Rosie's, except that it had a comfortable disorder instead of a sense of neurotic confusion. Some of the kids appeared to be asleep, while others were watching the financial news on television.

"The market was cautiously up again," the announcer was saying, and somewhere a boy snored softly. The program seemed a mildly ironic choice for parolees. No one paid the slightest attention to Keeny.

Beyond an arched opening, in the architectural style of a forgotten day, was a dining room. Two large tables nearly filled the room. At one of them sat Mr. Baker and an attractive red-haired woman. Mr. Baker was eating and the woman was talking to him. She gave Keeny a look that somehow united cynicism and welcome. Her smile said:

I've been snowed by experts, so don't try.

Mr. Baker glanced over his shoulder at Keeny. "Oh, hello!" he said. "Peggy this is Keeny Durán. Keeny, Mrs. Sherwood." He gave Keeny the homely grin he remembered from their brief meeting in the State building after he got out.

Keeny said hello, and the landlady turned a chair for him. "Sit down. I'll get you some dinner. Help yourself to coffee."

Keeny took a chair across from Mr. Baker. Mrs. Sherwood brought a plate of meat loaf and vegetables and he began eating hungrily, darting glances now and then at the front room. The presence of the girls puzzled him. In all the halfway houses he had seen, girls and persons infected with the plague were absolutely barred.

Mr. Baker talked about the operation of the house, saying more or less what he had said over the telephone that day, that the boys set most of their own rules, except that Mrs. Sherwood had the last word on some things. Keeny put most of it down as loose talk.

What about drugs, for instance? Drugs were the big scene where parolees were concerned, and if the guys here had records, then most of them were dropping pills or shooting up.

Period.

So maybe the house was full of dudes who knew how to fake out the P.O. and the landlady. But he was still puzzled about how it worked.

"Do you have girl parolees here, too, Mrs. Sherwood?" he asked.

"One of the girls is my daughter," said the landlady. "The others are friends of the boys."

Mr. Baker started filling a blemished meerschaum pipe. He was a big man with a strong nose, dark eyes, and thin, dark hair carelessly brushed over his scalp. In a suit of brown material that shone like a mole's coat, he looked like a successful businessman.

"Keeny, why did you wait to call me until you knew you couldn't take it any longer?" he asked.

"Man, it just piled up on me that night! And when I knew they were going to bust me, I decided I might as well run. You believe me about Armando, don't you?"

"Sure. But if I didn't, I'd still be interested in helping."

Keeny was puzzled. He had not really expected the P.O. to believe him. In fact, a lot of things about Mr. Baker and this strange parolee house baffled him.

"Excuse me, but what's the deal here?" he asked. "Who really makes the rules?"

"Actually, I figure the fewer the rules, the fewer the hassles over them. Some of the boys are probably getting loaded regularly. That's between them and the police, unless a guy lets me see him loaded. Then I'd have to ask him to live somewhere else, or it could mean my job."

Keeny relaxed. He had it figured out, now: The ones who lived here were very low-risk delinquents, carefully chosen from Mr. Baker's files. Probably one-time offenders. Blue-ribbon studs.

But a moment later, as if he had read Keeny's mind, the parole officer said: "We've got a pretty good cross-section of offenders here. I'm not interested in helping boys who don't need help. Most parolees go home when they get out, like you did. But if there isn't a home, or if it's unsuitable, then I have to put a boy somewhere else. Unfortunately, there aren't enough somewhere elses. So if Peggy's got space when an emergency comes up, I put the guy here, unless there's heroin or arson in his record. Heroin addicts need a kind of supervision we can't give them, and arsonists like to warm their hands at little fires we can't afford."

Keeny finished the pie. *So maybe the house was on the level,* he thought. *Maybe nobody was snowing anybody.* In his heart, however, he knew that was impossible.

"I guess it's time we got started," Mr. Baker said.

"On what?" Keeny asked.

"We have a special meeting here once a week. I'd like to get the boys on your case tonight. Okay?"

Keeny raised his hands palms-up. "What for, man? What good would it do?"

"Somebody might say something that would make sense to you. Okay?"

Keeny muttered, "Okay." What the hell, he owed them that much for the dinner.

Chapter 18

Boys began taking seats in the long, dusky front room. Someone switched off the television set. A lamp was turned on. Keeny heard boys clattering down an outside stairway from the upper floors of the old house. Soon they came drifting in through the front door. Finally about fifteen boys had gathered, in addition to the two adults and three girls. About half the boys were *chicanos.*

Sitting in a straight-backed chair beside Mr. Baker, who occupied a demolished armchair with red upholstery, Keeny studied the boys with quick, appraising glances. No one paid much attention to him. The boys were bumming cigarettes off each other and lighting up. The big boy with the long hair sat pensively jabbing a pin into the arm of the couch where he sat. He wore a cowboy hat and a long corduroy jacket.

In the dining room, out on the very frontier of the group, an outpost but not part of it, sat a Mexican boy with a mustache, a cut on the nose, and a raspberry-colored bruise involving all of one eye.

"Any matters you'd like to bring up, Peggy?" Mr. Baker said.

"Yes," said the landlady. "Andy is still working for All-American Bum. I think we'd better make it clear that if he's just using this house as a crash pad, we can use his bed for somebody who really needs it."

The big boy in the cowboy hat looked up with an indignant expression. "I'm going to school tomorrow, Peggy! I told you."

"And before that," said Mrs. Sherwood, "you told me you were going today."

"Well, you didn't get me up in time."

"Wayne woke you up at six, before he went to work. How early do we have to get you up?"

"I went back to sleep," Andy argued, jabbing the pin into the chair arm. "You have to check on me."

"No, we don't," Mrs. Sherwood said. "But *you* have to go to school, or work, or we'll have to have your bed. This has been going on for two months."

Andy raised both arms helplessly. His snub-nosed, freckled features showed outrage. "That's all in the past! I live in the present, Peggy. I *told* you, I'm going tomorrow!"

"And you told me yesterday you were going today."

"But I went back to sleep. Jeez!" Andy looked at the others in bafflement.

Keeny grinned. The logic was beautiful. The most beautiful part of all was that Andy probably believed every word of it. He was, apparently, one potential loser they had failed to screen out.

Mr. Baker kicked off some discussion of Andy's living in the future, rather than in the past. It seemed to him, he said, that you carried your past like a knapsack, whether you liked it or not. Youth Authority was getting tired of paying board on a guy who didn't work or go to school.

The cigarette smoke thickened. The P.O. glanced at the Mexican boy with the bruised face, who, with closed eyes, sat with his profile turned to the group. Though technically part of it, he sat outside the circle.

It looked to Keeny like a way of saying, *I'm here, but only because I have to be.*

"Manny," said the parole officer, "why don't you move in here with us?"

"This is okay," Manny muttered.

"Peggy says you had a bummer yesterday."

Manny, his eyes still closed, said: "No, man, it wasn't a bummer. I just fell downstairs."

"What happened?"

"I tripped."

None of the boys changed expression, but Mrs. Sherwood laughed. "You were loaded, Manny. We could hardly get you on your feet."

Manny opened his eyes for a moment to look at her. "All I did was take my medicine, Peggy. That's all."

"The doctor prescribed two of those pills a day for your epilepsy, not seven at a time. Do you take the other medicine he gave you? The dilantin?"

"It doesn't help. All that helps is my own medicine."

"Manny," said Mr. Baker, "your medicine is reds, so don't snow us. Why did you take them? Do you remember?"

Manny mumbled something inaudible.

A tall, thin boy with dark hair and slightly Oriental eyes spoke up. "Manny thinks we don't like him."

Manny shifted his chair a little farther from the circle. "Man, listen, I couldn't care less whether you like me! Nobody here likes me, Shelly, but that doesn't matter."

"Then why don't you move?" asked Shelly.

Manny drew on his cigarette. He had strangely smooth, vivid features, the eyes, eyebrows, and mustache very distinct. His bruised eye stood out like a blob of sherbet.

"Because I like it here," he said.

"Then why did you take all those downers?" Andy argued.

Manny pushed the sleeves of his sweater to the elbows and got up. "Get off my case, will you?" he said. He walked to a Coke machine in the corner. There followed the click and clank of his dropping a dime and uncapping a bottle. The room remained silent until he came back. He sat down, faced off again at right-angles to the group, and closed his eyes.

"Manny," Mr. Baker persisted, "have you ever had a real, close friend?"

"Man, I don't *need* close friends!" Manny protested. But presently he added, "Andy and I get along okay."

"Can I say something, Manny?" Keeny said.

Manny looked blankly at him.

"I know how you felt when you took those downers," Keeny said. "Because I did the same thing the other day. I was way down, man, all the way. Going it alone is like being in solitary, ain't that so?"

Manny lifted one shoulder.

"Then," continued Keeny, "I got somebody I could rap to. And things got better. So I was just thinking, the next time you get down, why not rap to Andy?"

"Yeah, okay," said Manny. "Thanks. Big deal."

Mr. Baker came in quietly: "I'm surprised to hear you say that you've got somebody you can rap to, Keeny. Who is it?"

Keeny cleared his throat, rubbed his jaw, and thought it over swiftly. Not that anybody could help, he thought. But they couldn't hurt, either. So, okay! Why not rap to them about how it was with Keeny Durán?

So he did.

Chapter 19

Keeny told them everything but where he was living—
even told them about 'Miliano. He thought that would
jar them, but Shelly said:

"That's like those voices Bob used to hear."

"Who's Bob?" asked Keeny.

Shelly grinned. "He went back to the joint. Dyer
Act."

"It's not like Bob at all," said the landlady. "*His*
voices used to egg him on to do things he shouldn't,
like stealing that car. Keeny's voice is trying to keep
him out of trouble."

Mr. Baker puffed on his pipe. "You've heard of the
dark side of the moon, Keeny? 'Miliano may be the
dark side of your mind. You don't see it often, but it's
there. And now, with things completely messed up, it's
come into the light to help you. It's telling it like it is."

"But, if it's my own mind," Keeny argued, "how
come 'Miliano knows things I don't? I didn't know that
Zapata started a revolution on March 11, 1911. I didn't
know his name was written in gold in the Chamber
of Deputies. How do you figure that?"

"Sure," Andy agreed, "how could the dummy talk
about things Keeny doesn't know himself? Unless
there's some other lash-up—"

The parole officer snorted. "You guys!" he said.
"Now you're telling ghost stories."

All at once they were all arguing with him, assaulting his solid practicality with guesses and theories. The girls, particularly, thought Keeny had something very special going. Keeny grew uneasy, remembering the way Yo-Yo had caught fire on the mystical aspect of 'Miliano.

"Didn't you tell us your father was a great guy . . . *muy Mexicano, muy macho?*" Mr. Baker asked, outshouting the others.

"Yes—"

"So he probably told you stories about the Mexican heroes, right?"

"Man, that was a long time ago."

"Maybe so, but *I* remember the stories my father told me. Some of them were true, some he must have made up. Now, *your* father, Keeny, didn't like the way the *chicanos* were put down, made to feel they were second-class people, like some intelligent species of burro. He didn't want his son to grow up thinking that Mexicans were inferior to *anybody,* so he must have told you stories about the great heroes of the Mexican Revolution. Maybe about the famous outlaws, too, like Joaquín Murieta, in California. Maybe he named his son after that Joaquín—"

Keeny reflected. "Maybe," he muttered. "At least I remember that I—I loved him, and we were happy, until he died. After that things fell apart."

He told about how he had felt: deserted. Of how his mother had started putting locks on everything, and how demoralizing school was.

"They'd call us things like Spanish-Americans, and Latins—everything but Mexicans, so our feelings wouldn't be hurt. Man, I was *proud* of being a Mexican! My father taught me to be proud of *la raza!* And here the teachers were working six hours a day trying to knock it out of me."

And they were still doing it in school, the other boys agreed. Grammar school, junior high, high.

"Sure they are," said Mr. Baker. "So why don't you *chicano* guys get involved in trying to clean the mess up? Get in the Brown Berets, things like that. But don't forget one thing: Nobody's going to forgive you the mistakes you make today, just because you had an unhappy childhood. You're stuck with what you are, what you do. Responsibility, that's the name of the game. Like taking off after Armando got hurt. Man, you knew better than that. Whose fault was it, the Rock's?"

"You're playing his game, Keeny," Andy agreed. "The longer you hide, the worse it'll be when they find you."

"I can't see that I've got much to lose by waiting," Keeny retorted. "If I turn myself in, I get a pair of Juvie pants and the dumbest lawyer in the city. Some dude that thinks an over-parking rap is a big criminal case."

He got up. "Thanks for the dinner, Mrs. Sherwood. And thanks for trying, Mr. Baker."

"So what are you going to do?" Andy persisted. "Wait to be caught?"

Keeny hesitated, his hand on the doorknob. "Maybe, maybe not. Because I've already got a lawyer, and I'm waiting for him to tell me my move."

"Who's that?" asked Mr. Baker.

" 'Miliano," Keeny said.

Chapter 20

Throughout the next day he thought about Mr. Baker's theory of what made the general talk. If he was right, then something big must be going on down there in the locked dungeon of his soul; some masterplan was being nailed together from the scraps of disaster which were the life of Joaquín Durán. But if so, the general was taking his time about coming up with anything helpful.

Keeny placed the general on a table. As a sort of offering, he set before him Concha's jar of wilted geraniums. He combed his hair and washed his hands. Then, in as pure a state as he could achieve, he sat down before the general and closed his eyes.

"Okay, man! Let's go! What do I do?"

Nada, nada, was the general's answer. *Nothing.* From the dark side of his mind, the basement of his soul, came not a scrap of inspiration.

He wrinkled his brow, tried to turn off his mind like an engine, putting everything in Zapata's control. "Man, give! I believe, I believe! What comes next?"

Nothing.

No, not quite. Thoughts nibbled at his consciousness like mice. One had to do with a P.T.A. carnival Mousie had mentioned. *Okay—big deal! I'll go to the carnival and win some goldfish.* But this idea of the carnival kept coming back like a song he could not drive from his mind.

At nightfall he unlocked the side door in case anyone should come around. He was beginning to feel totally down. *What now, chicano? Take some reds?*

Then he heard a door open downstairs and the Aztecs came in quietly, by twos, all but Gato. Pelón sat beside Keeny and took him by the shoulders.

"Keeny, you've got to split! They picked Gato up night before last. I can't understand why he hasn't finked on you before this. We came to warn you last night, but you weren't here."

Keeny smiled. "If he told them where I am, they'd think he was hallucinating. If he talks, he talks. The hell with it."

Off in the night, a siren reached for a high note and held it, screaming like a bench-saw going through steel. The boys looked at Keeny. He shrugged.

"They howl all the time around here. It's the ones that come like a cat that worry me."

"One's coming, Keeny, one's on the way," said Pelón. "Gato's no hero. Where are you going to be when the Man comes?"

"Where will I spend eternity?" Keeny said.

"I'm only saying that you'd better make up your mind. By now the Rock will be holding that hypodermic needle up to Gato and saying, 'One word gets you a *gramo*, Gato: *Where's he at?*'"

"Ask the dummy what to do," suggested Mousie.

They stared at the dummy as if expecting a Messiah-like pronouncement. But except for the fading, far-off scream of the siren, the room was silent.

"The general," stated Keeny, "doesn't know anything I don't. I was talking to Mr. Baker last night. He says I'm just feeding stuff back from my unconscious mind. Like maybe my old man used to tell me stories about the revolutionary heroes. Maybe that's where I learned about Zapata."

The boys waited, glancing from the general to Keeny and back again. At last Pelón said, fatalistically,

"Time's wasting, *camarada*. Better make up your mind what you're going to do."

In the silence, then, 'Miliano began to speak. The words were slow and forceful, and as Keeny heard them he shuddered in terror.

Joaquín will give himself up at the P.T.A. carnival! said the general.

"Wait a minute!" Keeny protested. "Just wait one—"

Joaquín will call his parole officer and tell him. Mr. Baker will ask Sergeant Rock to treat him like any other offender.

Keeny's will began to leak out of him. "Why at the carnival? What's the deal? All I want is a lawyer, a good one—"

You'll get a lawyer, said the general.

Keeny made a slashing gesture. "Don't rap to me about turning myself in, 'Miliano, not after what happened to you! They killed you in that village, remember?"

Perhaps I had to become a martyr to finish my work.

"What about *my* work? I haven't even started on it."

Pelón's hand closed on his arm. "Man, you'd better listen to him! Remember the night we didn't?"

"Yeah, but it's *me* saying it! It has to be!"

"Okay, it's you! So what? You know the odds better than anybody else, don't you? You know what you can do, and what you can't."

"Yeah, Pelón, I know! And I know that's one thing I'm not *about* to do!"

Impatiently, he shoved them to the door. Pelón gave him a grin from the stairs. "Sure, man. Do your thing. But call me when you want a ride to the school."

Chapter 21

Shaken, Keeny turned to 'Miliano. "Give myself up, huh? Man, I'll give you up!" He laid the dummy face down on a table. First he broke off the general's head. Then he snapped off his arms, and both legs in their tight leather pants. He tore the cardboard body lengthwise, ripped the pieces crosswise, and made a little heap of the torn paper.

The fragments silently accused him.

He ran to a window and managed to raise it a few inches in its rusty tracks. Then he carried the pieces of cardboard to the window. Shoving them through the bars one by one, he watched them go sailing and spinning away on the night wind. Some landed among the cars plowing up and down Chicago Street.

Closing the window, he went to his cell and lay on the bunk, trying to understand where, in this universe of stars and sewage, garbage and roses, joy and triumph, the atom bearing the name of Joaquín Durán was now traveling.

Then, at the very core of his being, he felt a seed of light begin to glow. The seed kept swelling, sending out roots and leaves of light. In his body a tingling commenced. Slowly, as he lay self-hypnotized and expectant, relief came to him, as cool as a mountain brook.

'Miliano was gone, but he had left something of himself behind: an insight, a clear and honest perception of how things were. Keeny knew now that the light had always been there, turning in the darkness like a beacon, illuminating his inmost being. When he had sprinted like an inspired Skid Row derelict—that was a flash from the beacon, a beam of hope. When he had tried to kill his fear with pills, that was the dark interval between flashes.

Would it always be that way? Up and down? Light and dark? Well, if it was, there would always be the flash after the darkness—if he waited.

Okay! he thought. *I turn myself in.*
I keep my cool and wait.
I use my head.
I listen.
Okay!

Sergeant Rock could hear two rookie cops talking in the hall outside his office.

"If you work it right," said one of them, "maybe you'll make lieutenant. Paste those pieces of cardboard together and tell the captain you've solved the Great Display-Dummy Mystery."

"Well, I mean, it's no big deal," said the other officer, whose voice betrayed that despite all he was rather proud of himself. "I just happened to remember hearing a call the other night from Metro Division. It was about a dummy stolen from a theater. I don't know how it got on the air, it's such small potatoes. So I'm driving down Chicago Street ten minutes ago, and a piece of cardboard slams into my windshield! I stop to eyeball things, and I see some other pieces in the street, and pretty soon I know it's the dummy!"

"I'll tell you what you do," said the first officer.

"You get yourself a carton about so big—you know? And you put all these pieces in it. And then you shove it."

"Collins!" said Sergeant Rock.

A fresh-faced young officer stepped into the Rock's doorway. He carried a sheaf of torn cardboard slabs under his arm:

"Yes, sir!"

"What are you talking about?" asked the Rock.

Officer Collins went through the recital again.

"Where did this happen?" asked the sergeant.

"Two blocks up the street."

"Let me see the stuff."

Rock fitted two pieces of paper together. The face of Emiliano Zapata glared up at him from his desk.

"This was reported stolen, huh?"

"Yes, sir. From a Skid Row theater."

"You found it on Chicago Street?" Rock rotated his cigar between his lips, his eyes reflective.

"Yes, sir. I figured somebody'd thrown them from a moving car, and that I plowed into one that was still floating."

"Probably. Okay. Thanks."

The sergeant, dressed in a sharp, dark suit, his well-barbered jaws pallid, put on a small-brimmed hat and checked out. He liked to drive and think. Cruising the area, he saw a couple of pieces of the dummy that Collins had missed, lying in the middle of an intersection near the old police station.

The Rock focused his mind on the problem.

Why, if Durán had stolen it, would he have torn it up?

Who but Durán, of course, would steal such a thing? Who but a guy all messed up with Mexicanism? College kids stole trash barrels, street signs, red lanterns. Why wouldn't a kid like Durán steal a

Mexican revolutionary general for his pad, wherever it was?

He's telling us something, thought Rock. *What's he saying? Where is he?*

He gazed along the shabby street, garish with many-colored neon signs, blinking with lights that emphasized its poverty, like the jingling costume jewelry on a Skid Row hustler. Reflectively he stared at the dark police station.

I ought to get the keys to that old barn, he thought. *I could think better in there.*

But he dropped the idea. Most of the furniture had been moved from it, nearly everything worth carrying away. It would merely make him sad to roam again the rooms grimed with the lives of a hundred thousand forgotten felons, impressing him with the contrast between police work fifteen years ago and the way it was today, hamstrung by civil rights groups and the Supreme Court.

No, Sergeant Rock decided. It would be better not to go back. As Durán would say, going back would be a bad scene.

He returned to the station to call Juvenile Hall and learn whether Gato had started talking yet.

Chapter 22

Keeny made his calls the next night:

To Pelón, asking him to pick him up at exactly two o'clock Saturday in the alley behind the police station.

To Frank Baker, telling him he was going to turn himself in soon, and please check with Juvenile Hall Saturday night if he had not been notified.

Even to his home, where he talked to Estela while his mother shrieked at Carlos and Armando in the background, and yelled at 'Stel to get off the phone if she were talking to "that boy, that rapist, that Guillermo. . . ." Thoughtfully Keeny hung up, having learned two things:

That Armando was recovering nicely, able to be yelled at again.

And that he could never, never go home again.

Life had made his mother the way she was: But she was making her kids what they were. He had followed her road as far as he could, and now he was plunging into the thickets in search of his own destiny. Away from her, he could be sorry for her, could even help a little, perhaps. Penned up with her, he could only hate and fight her. In a year he would be eighteen and could live wherever he wanted—providing he got out of the joint within a year. Providing he did not draw an adult sentence and go in with those animals who made queers and junkies and weirdos out of a kid.

On Saturday morning he shaved and took a sponge bath at the galvanized-iron sink, like a Marine getting ready for a landing.

Having time to kill, he re-read some of the old newspapers and came across a story he had read before. The account blew a bugle in his head. He laughed aloud, and swatted his thigh with the paper.

The story about the kids in the southern school who fell asleep—a whole schoolful of them! Waves of gooseflesh traversed his arms and inspiration surged up from the darker, deeper level of his mind.

That's it! That's it! he thought.

At one-thirty he combed his hair neatly and got the red poncho out of the closet. And there on the floor of the closet, lying in a dark corner, he found the key to the whole operation: the dynamite to blow the Rock right off his chair.

A square-shouldered little brown bottle in a corner. According to the label, the bottle had once contained one hundred five-grain aspirin tablets, no doubt for headaches inflicted on the police by the doings of such people as Joaquín Durán. Though empty, the bottle was capped, with a residue of white dust in the bottom of it.

Keeny slipped it in his pocket. If it would work in the South, why not here?

He went downstairs to meet Pelón.

The moment he reached the alley, a car engine started up a hundred feet away. Pelón drove up, alone, his old car enveloped in blue smoke. Keeny slid in beside him. *"Todo madre!"* said Pelón. At the north end of the alley he turned east, then doubled south at the next block and worked back to Arroyo Street before turning toward Happy Valley.

He glanced at Keeny, looking sad but resigned. "It's the only route to go, man," he said.

Keeny said cheerfully: "That's what I know. I'm counting on you for some help, though."

"Sure. What kind?"

Keeny told him.

Pelón massaged the back of his neck with one hand. He did not see how Keeny's idea was going to help, he said, but he was willing to go along with him on it. Anything for a friend.

They crossed a bridge, climbed a long slope, and turned south into the jungle of tarpaper-roofed dwellings on the heights above Happy Valley. Cars were parked everywhere along the streets, and families, from babes-in-arms to parents, were hurrying toward Cabrillo Elementary School.

Pelón wedged his car into a space in an alley and they walked among other kids and adults toward the school. Over the neighborhood floated the sounds of music. Below the ridge, half-hidden by trees, Keeny made out the geometrical shapes of the housing project. He knew, with a feeling of sadness, that he would never go back there again. That home was burned. Where he would go from here depended on how things went at the carnival in the next hour.

They passed along the high cyclone fence with its unforgiving barbed-wire topping. Keeny saw brown-paper carnival booths set up against the buildings along one side of the playground. The day was hot and dry, with dust in the air. Everyone seemed to be carrying a paper cup or a sno-cone.

Two *chicano* fathers were on duty at the main gate, not selling tickets but eyeballing the guests for potential troublemakers. One of them frowned at Keeny and Pelón, and said, "No trouble, now."

"No trouble," they said. They went inside.

The school consisted of a core of very old stucco buildings, lead-gray and streaked, augmented by wooden barrackslike buildings that the school district moved from school to school, like trailers, as enrollment rose and fell. From the auditorium in the old building Keeny heard the hard-banging screech and wail of a high school musical group. There seemed to be a million little kids darting around licking popsicles, eating tacos, waving plastic propellers and screaming. Mothers screamed after them and fathers stood in little embarrassed groups talking and getting up nickels and dimes as the kids checked in with them.

A man's voice bawled over the public address system:

"We've got a lot of good food here and it's priced right! Don't forget the drawing at four o'clock for the Mixmaster. Be sure and drop your ticket stub in the box at the gate."

Keeny and Pelón kept circulating. Sooner or later, Keeny knew, a police car would arrive and the fuzz would saunter in and look around. He had things to do before they arrived. Mousie and Apache drifted up.

"Don't stick too close," Keeny murmured, "but keep an eye on me. Are the other guys here?"

"*Simón!*" said Apache.

"We'll get some Kool-Aid first," Keeny said. "As soon as I've got mine, you guys come up and get yours."

Some high school kids recognized him on the way to the Kool-Aid stand. They stared. "Hey, man!" said a kid named Lopez, from Keeny's English class. "You better split. The cops were here fifteen minutes ago. They asked if we'd seen you."

"I'll be careful," Keeny said.

Impressed, the kids watched him and Pelón move off. Keeny knew the word was going around. Just like Zapata going into that village alone to meet his fate! By the time he reached the booth where punch was being sold from a big aluminum army kettle, he was aware of half the carnival crowd watching him. Two women were dispensing punch into paper cups.

"Yes, how many?" asked a small woman.

Keeny stared up at the sky, shading his eyes against the sun. He gave Pelón the elbow.

"Police helicopter! They really keep an eye on this Cabrillo crowd," he said.

The women gazed up. While they were searching for the imaginary helicopter, Keeny took one of the ladles and gave the punch a stir. Looking down just then, one of the women caught him at it.

"Keep your hands away! It's the food laws," she warned. "I don't see any helicopter," she added.

Keeny grinned. "Maybe it's something I drank. I thought I saw a helicopter. Give us each a cup of that punch, *señora.*"

She gave him a hard eye. "Ten cents."

As he walked off, the brown aspirin bottle fell from his hand to the blacktop pavement. It bounced and spun. The woman who had taken his money stared at it in disapproval. "What *is* that?"

"Oh, that's just an empty aspirin bottle," Keeny said innocently.

"Aspirin!" The woman picked it up. Seeing that it was empty, she set it on the table. "If the police come back, we'll see whether it was aspirin or not!"

As Keeny and Pelón strolled away, the other Aztecs came toward the drink stand.

Keeny let fifteen minutes pass. Then he said to Pelón, "Let's go!"

They started back to the drink stand at a high and floating gait. Keeny had been loaded often enough to know how to fake it. He bumped into Pelón, and both of them started giggling. They got straightened out and pretended to become very sober, like drunks faking sobriety. Pelón made loose-wristed passes at imaginary butterflies floating about his head. By the time they reached the drink stand, Keeny was shivering, and he looked vaguely at the woman who had waited on him before.

"Yes, what is it?" she asked. It was clear that she disapproved of boys like them.

"Uh, uh," he said. He looked at Pelón. Apache, Goyo, and Mousie had appeared also. "Man, wha' we come here for?"

"They're loaded, they're loaded!" whispered the first woman to the other.

"You boys get out," said the second woman. "Just get out, leave the school grounds! If you aren't gone in one minute we'll call the police. It's disgusting!"

"Go' be lot of other guys loaded," said Apache. And he began laughing and making swimming motions with his arms, as though he were treading water.

"Hey, man, I feel—I feel like—" Goyo seemed trying to focus his eyes on the punch. "Feel like—I don't know. What was in that Kool-Aid? Acid?"

Both women stared at the punch kettle. Then the shorter one picked up the aspirin bottle, still sitting there, and uttered a shriek.

"*Acid! Oh, my God!*" She clenched her fists and shook them at Keeny. "What did you put in the punch, you—you addict! *What did you do?*"

Keeny fumbled out a couple of quarters and laid them on the table. "I'm setting them up for my friends.

Whoooee! Listen, this here is—I mean—like *wow!*"

One of the women ran toward a table where a man sat with a microphone, huckstering over the P.A. system for the various booths and chances.

The Aztecs worked out into the scattered crowd, dazed and stumbling. Mousie fell to the ground and began fighting off an opponent only he could see, while he screamed. Lopez came up to Keeny.

"What's happening, man?" he said anxiously. He carried a slightly wrinkled paper cup of punch in his hand.

Keeny looked through and beyond him. "Beautiful scene," he said. "That Kool-Aid! Oh, man! Somebody musta put acid in it! Ain't it hit you yet?"

At that moment the volume soared on the P.A. system and the announcer began shouting:

"*Atención, por favor!* Your attention, please! Anyone who has purchased punch in the last half-hour, *do not drink it!* Anyone who has already drunk it, please—" Running out of material, stricken with the monstrousness of what had happened, the man finished, "—please sit down in the shade if you feel dizzy. There is a chance that the punch was—was not good."

Then, to be sure that everyone understood, he repeated the warning in Spanish.

Chapter 23

Keeny sat on a bench in the shade and watched the carnival fly apart. Mexican mothers, trying to collect their small fry, screamed and tottered about, going out of their minds.

LSD in the Kool-Aid! All my kids have been drinking it! I drank three cups myself. Those addicts! My God, I'm dizzy!

He saw two mothers trying to comfort another woman who sat on the ground shrieking. Kids were pouring out of the auditorium, half of them with paper cups in their hands.

What's going on? What's all that about the Kool-Aid? Man, what's happening?

A teen-age girl from Keeny's school suddenly put both hands to her cheeks and began wailing, then fainted. A group of boys were hallucinating. *Acid in the Kool-Aid, man! Thought it seemed kind of hot in there! Hey, ain't that a ring around the sun? Yeah, man, and there's music coming out of it!*

The announcer was whipping people into a frenzy with his exhortations to keep cool. Once he advised putting the finger down the throat to empty the stomach, but fortunately no one seemed to hear him. Keeny lay on his back on the bench in the warm, dusty shade and listened to the uproar. Pelón came by, languidly grabbing at butterflies.

"How long we got to keep on doing this?" he asked.

"Few more minutes. When you hear the sirens, you guys better split."

"What about you?"

"That's the whole idea," Keeny said. "I'm waiting for the Rock."

Pelón floated on.

Yet it seemed to take hours for the police to arrive. By the time the first siren wailed over the hills, twenty or thirty people were stretched out on the blacktop. Others, in various degrees of hysteria, were swaying, staggering, and crawling about the playground. Here and there a few men who had not drunk any punch were helping women and girls to places in the shade where they could lie down. The older boys seemed to be able to live with their hallucinations better than the girls and women. The smaller children were merely dazed. As far as that went, Keeny reflected, most of the older kids had tried drugs at some time, and were probably happily waiting for the full effect to reach them.

Then he heard the sirens.

Later there were cops running.

After some time, a couple of officers tracked him down. They yanked him to his feet and shoved him against the peeling stucco wall of a building. Keeny knew one of them, a big juvenile officer, swarthy, with a hook nose and a mouth like a hyphen beneath the blade of his nose. His name was Sergeant Arabian.

"Durán! What the hell's going on?" he demanded.

Keeny blinked, perfectly normal now. "Don't know, Sergeant! I've been asleep."

"Well, by God, you little grease-ant, I'll bet I can wake you up!"

Arabian had the handcuffs onto Keeny's wrists in a few swift movements. "Ouch," Keeny said.

"All right, let's have it," said the sergeant.

"I don't dig it!" Keeny remonstrated. "What's wrong with everybody?"

Arabian glared fiercely at him as though he might hit Keeny in the face. But he calmed himself. And suddenly a lithe big man dressed in a sharp gray suit came trotting up. He was tall, pale-faced, icy-eyed.

The Rock had arrived.

Sergeant Rock was wild. He kept both hands on Keeny's shoulders and his eyes drilled into his brain.

"DURÁN, WHAT THE HELL IS THIS?" he shouted.

"I don't know, Sergeant! It's weird, ain't it? I've just been hanging around."

"WHAT FOR?" A gust of the Rock's breath was sour with cigar-chewing.

"To turn myself in."

"OH, YEAH? WHY HERE?" Sergeant Rock was almost gasping for breath.

"Why not?" Keeny asked. "I figured it was time."

A patrolman came trotting up, red-faced and perspiring, holding in his hand the brown aspirin bottle. "Sergeant, here's the bottle the lady said—"

"HOLD IT WITH A HANDKERCHIEF, STUPID! I WANT IT TESTED FOR PRINTS—"

"It's mine, all right," Keeny said mildly. "I brought some aspirin along for a headache, and I dropped the bottle over by the drink stand after it was empty."

"Aspirin, eh?" said the Rock. "DURÁN, YOU MOTHER, I'LL SEE YOU IN LEAVENWORTH FOR THIS!"

"But it was only—"

"TAKE HIM TO THE STATION, BOOK HIM, AND SEND HIM STRAIGHT TO JUVIE!" bellowed the sergeant.

The red disaster truck from the fire department rolled in with a dying bulldog-growl as they shoved Keeny into the back seat of a police cruiser. Off they rolled.

Little time was wasted at the Glass House. Keeny was booked, mugged, and printed.

"I want a lawyer," he said, as he wiped his inky fingers on the two-square-inch piece of tissue they gave him.

"Oh, you'll get a lawyer, Durán," said the booking sergeant. "Would you believe Melvin Belli?"

"And I want to make a telephone call. I'm entitled to one."

"No, no," said the sergeant. "That's for human beings. We've booked you as an animal. Acid in the Kool-Aid! Couldn't you have slipped some heroin into a baby's bottle?"

"But I didn't—"

"Oh, we *know* that!" said the officer. "Nobody lies to the *po*lice. That's the whole foundation on which we've built our organization."

When they had completed the formalities, they loaded Keeny into the back of a police car, handcuffed, with two officers in the front seat and a heavy grille between the seats so that he could not attack them. They headed north on a freeway toward the marvelous new Juvenile Hall out in the Valley, that the kids called Disneyland North.

Chapter 24

Away out in the Valley, among olive groves and big, gray boulders, stood the new Juvenile Hall, wide and one-storied like the island fortress of some Caribbean dictator. In a winy sunset, the officers led Keeny to the big glass doors where a small television camera, mirror-faced, oval in shape, beamed down on them. The door slid open with a quick, impatient sigh of compressed air.

After that, Keeny could have written the script from the old Juvie pictures he knew so well.

The cops left him in the holding room, a glass cube full of benches. With five other boys, he waited to be processed.

After some time, an officer led him out to a desk where a secretary transferred his entire essence—all but his soul—to a four-by-six card. He surrendered money, wristwatch, and the peso-on-a-chain and got a receipt for them. And now, in a way, nothing remained of Keeny Durán but that receipt. If it were lost, he guessed he would cease to exist.

A very fat black probation officer led him down a mile of linoleum glistening like waxed butterscotch. Another overworked door sighed in vexation and let them through, after still another camera had eyeballed them. In the check-in room, off the next mile of butterscotch floor, the attendant said:

"Strip."

Keeny undressed. They stuffed his clothes into a green plastic bag and dumped his shoes in on top of them to make certain everything came out properly wrinkled. Then, on command, he got into a bathtub and bathed. Three honor-unit boys working under the direction of an officer were handing out prison clothing. Drying off, he was told:

"Muss up your hair."

Nude and shivering, he mussed it up and the P.O. searched it for pills. The same keen eyes scrutinized his ears, mouth, and nostrils for pills, and that was not the end of the search.

How come, Keeny wondered dismally, *I thought it would go any different?* How could a picture with the same old start have a different ending? He was suddenly discouraged.

They gave him a pair of baggy blue denims and a tee shirt about right for Armando. "The shirt's too small," he said.

"Twist it like a rope and pull on it," the attendant advised.

After treatment, the misshapen shirt fitted him like two yards of old dishtowel. He laced up some dirty black tennis shoes. Now he looked just right. Now the image was that of the born loser: hair on end, clothing as ugly as possible, toes cramped by too-small shoes and socks. Brain cramped by the closing trap. *Give up!* the system said. *Give up!* the prison clothes, smell, and feel cried out.

Carrying a towel and blanket, he went out into the hall and sat on a bench with some younger boys to wait. Two boys who had recognized each other were comparing stories on how they had come to Juvie this time. They were about twelve.

"What comes next?" Keeny asked them.

"Unit Eighty," a boy with long blond hair said.

"What's that?"

"Man, don't you know nothing?" jeered the wise child. "That's the reception room. You'll get assigned a room and stuff. Don't mouth off or they'll shove you in an Iso room."

Keeny told him coldly, "Man, don't you know Iso's the only place where you can get privacy in a joint? I always go that route."

"Hey, that's right," said a black youngster about ten years old. "I always been sleeping on the floor because the beds are full in Unit Five Hundred. I guess I'll go that route too."

In Unit 80, Reception, an intake P.O. explained his rights.

"Your mother has been informed and states that she wishes you to have a court-appointed attorney. Mr. Weeden will visit you tomorrow morning."

"What's wrong with Mr. Weeden?" asked Keeny.

"Nothing, why?"

"What's he doing here, then? Can't he make a living?"

"You talk like a kid that wants to go to an Iso room," retorted the P.O.

"I do, I do," Keeny said, with a sneer.

"Well, I think it can be arranged. Loomis, is there an Iso room free?"

"You bet," said the officer on duty. Suddenly there came a rattle of noise from a squawk-box and the officer pushed a button and held a brief conversation with an attendant at the other end of the wire.

"Okay," he said, releasing the button. To the intake P.O. he said, "Charlie Sams is high again. His roommate says he ate a can of nutmeg in the kitchen. Can you get high on nutmeg?"

"Sounds like Charlie Sams can," said the other man.

"Okay, Durán, on your feet. Pick up your towel and blanket, who do you think you are?"

The Isolation room was the nicest cell Keeny had had in years. He had it all to himself. There was a window of reinforced glass—painted brown—a toilet and washbowl, and about eight square fet of that delicious-looking linoleum. The cell had everything but a bed, as though an inmate might hang himself or something with a bed. Probably, when they had the building almost finished, everything but the roof installed, the money ran out and they had to do away with the idea of beds. Apparently the black boy had been wrong about there being beds in Iso.

He spread his blanket on the floor and lay down with his arms crossed under his head, and just purely thought. Hours passed. Faces kept coming and going at the portholelike window in the door. Once it was a group of college kids. He heard the words, "—ones who might be potential troublemakers for instance," before the group moved along.

He knew the college sociology crowd well, rather liked them. He used to say things to them like, *I ate thirty downers once and it never phased me, I'm so conditioned to them. What do you turn on to? I have this fantasy of setting fire to my pants. Can a minor boy be charged with contributing to the delinquency of a minor girl?*

He kept waiting for Mr. Baker to show up. When dinnertime came and he had not appeared, Keeny asked the P.O. who had charge of his unit, "How come my P.O. hasn't shown? His name's Frank Baker."

"Didn't they tell you? Baker's in Santa Barbara at a criminology convention."

In the morning the door to his cell sucked open with

a hiccup and the morning probation officer looked in. "Your lawyer, sir," he said.

Tables and chairs were bolted to the corridor floor outside the Iso rooms. Keeny sat on one side of a table and regarded the pitiful man on the other side. Mr. Weeden sat very small inside a suit of navy blue like that of a streetcar conductor, the material so shiny he probably had to dim it for approaching cars. He wore a yellow-gray hairpiece set askew on a tiny, florid head. His breathing was labored and noisy, like the rattle and hiss of a scuba diver working at two hundred feet. He was obviously in an early stage of death. He smiled nervously.

"They've got you charged with two counts of Section Six-Oh-Two, Joaquín," he said. "That's a delinquent *act*, not just a tendency, so—"

"That's okay. Only I'm innocent."

"I suppose so," Mr. Weeden wheezed. "But all the evidence is against you. So why don't you admit your guilt and we'll ask for probation?"

"I'm already on parole, so I couldn't get probation."

Mr. Weeden rummaged in a blue plastic briefcase. "Oh, are you? Yes, I see. Well, in that case, we'll just have to take our chances. . . . In the meantime, son, maybe you'd like to tell me what really happened at the schoolground?"

"It's all on the charge sheet, Mr. Weeden."

"Yes, but why did you do it?"

"Do what?"

"Put LSD in the punch?"

Keeny shook his head. "That's the whole point. I didn't."

"But you let them *think* you did. You went to a lot of trouble to make yourself look guilty. Why?"

"I'm saving that for the judge, Mr. Weeden. I wanted to see— Well, it's hard to explain. But I had a good reason."

Mr. Weeden began putting papers back in his portfolio. "Well, I won't press you. I'll ask for Judge Cilch, he's very lenient."

"He sent me to Deuell four years ago, Mr. Weeden. Haven't you looked at my file?"

"I just got it last night. There'll be a detention hearing tomorrow. Your best bet is to plead guilty and—"

"I *can't* plead guilty," Keeny said patiently. "I'm still a minor."

"That's true, but it's the same thing: Admit to what you're charged with and throw yourself on the mercy of the court."

"I think I'll go *pro per*," Keeny said. "Can I do that? Represent myself?" he added, not sure that Mr. Weeden would understand the term.

"Not as a minor."

"Well, thanks a lot, Mr. Weeden. I'll ask my P.O. to get my old attorney for me. He knows my case."

"All right, son."

Keeny lay down on the floor of his cell, feeling rather bad about Mr. Weeden, who looked as though he could probably use the money for defending him.

Chapter 25

It was Sunday, Visitor's Day. Keeny steeled himself for the moment of hysteria with his mother. But she never came. No one, in fact, showed up. Isolation was lonely. There was no television, baseball, nor other recreation. But the days in Chicago Street Police Department had helped prepare him for going it alone.

On Monday he was taken to a small classroom, where, with a dozen other boys, he was given psychological tests. He was getting pretty good on the tests, having had them so many times that he would look at the designs and say at once to himself, *Oh, the Ravens test again, I like that one*. He was homed in on most of the Ravens designs after all these years. He once scored Genius.

On Monday afternoon Mr. Baker showed up.

They sat at the bolted-down table in the hall and studied each other. Mr. Baker, too big for the small chair and pint-sized table, looked uncomfortable. He played with his stained meerschaum pipe but did not light it. His dark brown eyes brooded.

"I'm sorry I wasn't here last week," he said. "How are they treating you?"

"Fine. Got everything but a bed."

"That's the way it goes when you play games. What's all this new stuff I hear? Acid in the Kool-Aid! Man!"

"What did I do?" Keeny asked. "What do they say I did?"

"Look, I'm not going to play games with you, Keeny. You tell *me* what you did."

"Nothing. They just got all excited."

"The detention hearing will be tomorrow morning. If you can't tell the judge any more than that, you'll be held for a probation hearing, and probably go to Deuell."

Keeny nodded earnestly. "That's what I want. I want to tell the judge the whole story—"

"With witnesses? With the police, your mother, maybe Armando, plus any other victims they can scare up?"

"The whole deal," Keeny said. "I want to lay it on the line and ask the judge if I got a fair shake anywhere along the line."

Mr. Baker rubbed his forehead, where two long creases ran vertically into his hairline, like old saber scars. "Hell, I don't know. Maybe that's the best way to play it. Lay it on the line. What about an attorney?"

Keeny looked at his hands, lying on the table like two anatomical exhibits. He wiggled a couple of fingers to see if they still worked, were still attached to the rest of the equipment. *We have here the hands of Joaquín Durán. They work like anyone's, although they are attached to the body of a loser who, believe it or not, world, is tired of being told how to lose, and is going to lose on his own this time.*

"An old guy named Mr. Weeden interviewed me," he said.

"You might as well have Weeden as anybody, if you're going in with this kind of a case," said the parole officer. "But he's pretty bad."

"Okay. Will you tell him to show up?" It had occurred to Keeny that Mr. Weeden might be the perfect ringmaster for the kind of show he wanted to put on.

"All right. How are they treating you?"

"Fine. You already asked me that."

Mr. Baker smiled wearily. "Guess I did. I'm kind of disturbed. You've got a lot of class, Keeny, and I'd like to help. By the way, I've got to hand the judge a report on your latest activity. What shall I say about the acid incident?"

"Just say I didn't have anything to do with it. It's the truth!"

"Okay. It's only your life."

At ten-thirty the next morning, Keeny's door opened with a gasp. It was like science fiction, the way things operated around here. Even the lights went on and off at the touch of some distant button. He was lying on the floor looking very Juvie in baggy blue denims, black tennies, and a misshapen tee shirt.

"Your court appearance, sir," said the jovial morning attendant.

Keeny got up and combed his hair once more with the comb they had given him. "What judge did I draw?" he asked.

"Ted Closson."

"Is he lenient?" Keeny asked, as they started down the hall.

"Why, old Ted hasn't given anybody less than ten years since he was elected," said the probation officer. "They call him The Ten-Year Man. He told me once that his philosophy of delinquency was—how did he put it?—something about throwing away a key."

Keeny knew that was a crock. Juveniles received no sentence. The deal was either probation, or placement in this or that institution for an indeterminate time. In his case it would be revocation of parole, and placement.

Mr. Baker was talking to Mr. Weeden outside a room halfway down the corridor to Reception. He patted Keeny on the shoulder and let his hand rest there a moment.

"Your mother and Armando are here," he said. "Don't let her excite you, Keeny. Probably the less you say to her, the better.

"That's good advice," Mr. Weeden wheezed.

The courtroom was small, about the size of a large living room, with a few rows of seats and a desk at which Judge Closson sat flanked by a clerk and a bailiff. In wall-brackets behind him were two flags, the Bear Flag of California and the flag of the United States.

In the first row of seats Keeny saw his mother and Armando. Sergeant Arabian was present. The woman who had sold Keeny the Kool-Aid sat near the back of the room. There were some other people who he supposed had been at the P.T.A. carnival. At least he did not recognize them, so they were not from the Project.

"Better sit by your mother," murmured Mr. Baker. "It'll make a better impression."

Keeny drew a quick breath. He saw her head turn. Their eyes clashed like swords. As soon as he was seated, she began hissing at him.

"*Vergüenza!* To shame my face before the world!"

Keeny stared fixedly at the judge, trying to encapsulate himself in his own thoughts. The judge was a lean, middle-aged man with gray hair cut a half-inch long all over, and the look of an old track-man. You could see him wearing a sweatsuit or tennis clothes and perspiring. Judge Closson studied Keeny through professorial spectacles. Trying to nail him down by type, Keeny settled on firm-but-fair. He was about to try a little smile on him when he realized that the judge would no doubt consider a smile outrageous conning, so he decided on an expression of solemnity.

Then he had an inspiration.

He leaned forward so that he could see Armando, on the other side of his mother. "Hi, 'Mando!" he said. Armando, his arm in a cast, grinned at Keeny.

"Are you coming home?" he asked sweetly.

"Sure. Do you still love me, 'Mando?"

"Yes!"

Keeny's mother turned to Armando. "Shhh!" she said. *"Cállete!"*

Keeny winked at Mr. Baker. Maybe Armando wouldn't turn State's witness after all.

The clerk read from a paper and the judge glanced over a fat file of white, pink, and blue papers which were the record of Keeny Durán, neatly bound in paper-clamps.

"The petition," he said, "alleges that the defendant, Joaquín Durán, violated Section Six-Oh-Two of the Welfare and Institutions Code in that he maliciously pushed his brother out of a window; and further that he resisted arrest for this act. A second count under the same section alleges that the same Durán adulterated food or drink at a public place in such a manner that persons became intoxicated on a drug commonly known as LSD. Officer Wengle, do you want to tell us about Count One?"

Keeny had not recognized the young officer who had been one of the arresting officers at the Project. In street clothes, the man was sworn in and took a seat near the judge's desk.

He told about that night.

"Are there any witnesses?" the judge asked.

Keeny's mother said quickly, "Mrs. Ortega, my neighbor, Your Honor! She saw Armando fall right by her window—"

"Did she see him fall *from* your window?"

"No, sir! My God, how could she, she lives underneath us?"

The judge pulled up his lower lip, frowning. "Then there are no actual witnesses to what took place in the apartment?"

Keeny raised his hand. The judge nodded at him.

"Yes, sir," Keeny said. "Armando was there."

"I meant other than Armando. But since there don't seem to be any other eyewitnesses, I'll call the little boy. Do you want to sit beside me, Armando?"

Mrs. Durán led Armando to the chair. She tried to kneel beside it, but the judge sent her back to her place. He talked with Armando for a while about what he liked to do and what toys he had. Keeny's muscles locked up very tight.

"Do you like to sail paper airplanes?" asked the judge.

"No!" Armando's face puckered.

"Why not?"

Armando shook his head.

"Did you get hurt when you were sailing them once?"

Armando nodded, and Judge Closson asked interestedly, "What happened that night, Armando?"

"I falled out of the window!" Armando said, puckering up.

"And that's how you hurt your arm?"

Armando nodded, his lower lip thrust out.

"But the doctors are making your arm all right, aren't they? What made you fall, Armando?"

Keeny clutched the chair arms. He saw Armando look at their mother and grow confused.

"Tell the truth!" cried Mrs. Durán, standing up. "Tell about—"

"Don't guide him, Mrs. Durán," said Judge Closson sharply. "Sit down, please."

"But, Your Honor—"

"Mrs. Durán, sit down!" She did so, finally, weeping, and the judge touched Armando's arm and the boy looked into his face.

"What happened?"

"I just falled," Armando said.

Keeny sank back.

"Who made you fall? Who made you?" Mrs. Durán cried.

This is my mother? Keeny thought. This is my loving mother trying to get me sent to jail? If this is a mother, who needs an enemy?

"If you can't control yourself, Mrs. Durán," said the judge, "I'll ask you to leave. We've already had a pretty good answer to the question: He just fell. I think we'll have to accept it." The judge patted 'Mando and sent him back to his seat.

"Now, about the other charge, the LSD," he said. "Mrs. Herrerra, will you take the stand?"

The Kool-Aid lady was sworn in. She was prepared to tell a good one, Keeny saw—it was obvious from the back-fence-gossip delivery she started with. But the judge interrupted her frequently to ask whether she had *seen* Durán put something in the punch, or merely assumed it? And did she have any reason to believe the bottle was anything but an empty aspirin bottle? And what made her think that anything had been put in the punch at all?

"When the boys, those Aztecs, came back to the stand, they were all high!" she testified. "I've seen boys on drugs before, and these boys were *high*, Your Honor!"

"Had you seen anyone else acting high?"

Not up to then, she admitted. Just the Aztecs.

Judge Closson riffled papers and read something to himself. "The laboratory report," he said, "states that there was only a residue of aspirin in the bottle. There was nothing in the punch but the usual sweeteners and flavoring. So what started all this nonsense about LSD, Sergeant Arabian?"

Sergeant Arabian rose to his feet, a frown of anxiety on his large, dark, scimitar-nosed face.

"Well, as we got it, Your Honor, the Aztecs were showing evidence of being loaded. Then the announcement was made over the P.A. that there was something in the punch, and—well, it was like an epidemic. I'd say, now that I know the lab report, that the Aztecs were maliciously putting people on."

Judge Closson smiled. "I'm not sure there are degrees of putting people on, Sergeant. Joaquín, come forward and take the stand."

Chapter 26

"In your own words," said the judge, "what happened?"

Watching the court reporter's tape piling up in the box, Keeny told about the put-on. The facts were simply that he had bought some punch, pointed to the sky, stirred the punch, and came back later acting loaded. On his suggestion, his friends also pretended to be under the influence of narcotics.

"That's all," he concluded. "Is it against the law to put people on?"

The judge scrutinized him. "There is precedent for jailing someone for yelling 'fire' in a crowded theater," he said. "The two situations may not be the same, but they are certainly parallel. A case can be made for an illegal put-on, I'm sure."

Keeny frowned at his hands, linked in his lap.

"Why don't you tell us the truth, now," said the judge. "You staged a very elaborate show that might have resulted in people being hurt. You admit that. Suppose you tell us why?"

Keeny smoothed the wrinkled denim over his thighs. Then he looked at the judge, openly.

"I just wanted to see how far people would go to make it tough on you, when you were innocent. When there was no evidence at all against you. I wanted everybody to know. That's all. I wanted it to be a big show like that, so everybody in town would know about it."

"And what would that prove?"

"That would prove that once you've been in trouble, they get down on you and you don't have a chance. With me, the trouble started when I was seven. I've been in trouble ever since. Most of the time I was wrong. I couldn't stand it at home, and I'd take off, or bust a window or something, to get the feeling off me.

"But this last time it's been different. Ask them about my grades in school. I've been trying hard, Your Honor, and it wasn't easy. My mother—well, she's got a hard life, but so do I. We don't get along, and I asked my parole officer to find me a foster home. But he says there's no place to put teen-age delinquents but in prison, because nobody wants us."

"Unfortunately," said the judge, "that's about right."

Keeny looked at some of the faces. Mr. Baker's, solemn but encouraging. His lawyer's, half-asleep, the eyelids fluttering. The Kool-Aid lady, and the officers, trying to hold a certain expression of fairness-without-approval.

"So," he said, "since I had nothing to lose, I decided to go for broke. And I feel like I proved what I was trying to. At least I proved it to myself."

"Which was—?" the judge prompted, when he hesitated.

"Which was that you're guilty until proved innocent, once you've got a record. I did everything I was supposed to that night. I was afraid Armando would get hurt, and I was making him some toast when he fell out of the window. But Mrs. Ortega and the policemen put the shaft to me. Like one of the cops—the officers—said, 'Durán's an old-timer.' Sure I was. But that didn't make me guilty. I shouldn't have taken off, but I—I don't know—I decided, 'What the hell, they've already convicted me.' I ran so as to—well, I don't really know why I ran," he said, with a shrug.

Keeny's mother put her arm around Armando and pulled him close. Keeny winced. *The poor kid!* he thought. *She'll demolish him like she did me. It may be called love, but it comes on like poison. If I get out of this, she'll have me to fight before she messes him up. Some way, I'll be around.*

"Where did you get the LSD idea?" asked the judge.

Keeny told about the old newspaper story, which led him to 'Miliano. He was well into the story, and the judge was listening in fascination, when Mr. Baker stood up.

"Your Honor, I'd like to say something," he said.

Judge Closson recognized him with a gesture.

"This 'secret friend' phenomenon isn't too unusual, as you know," he said. "What impresses me about Keeny's imaginary friend, however, is that all the advice he had from him was good. 'Miliano read him the riot act when he did anything wrong. He even talked Concha into trying to straighten out. I called her parole officer this morning and got the good news that she's still in the work-home, going to church and school, and making something of herself. This wasn't one of those 'voices' that tells an individual to kill, to steal, to set fires. This was Joaquín's own conscience, and I just want to point out that it was at least as good as mine."

He looked at Keeny.

"I feel, as I said in my report, that he deserves another chance. If we're interested in rehabilitation, here's a beautiful chance to help one boy rehabilitate."

"Do you know the meaning of 'rehabilitate'?" asked the judge.

"Yes, sir. 'To restore to a former capacity.'"

"The defendant's chief capacity has been for trouble, hasn't it?"

"Yes, sir. But most of that trouble has grown out of home conflicts. That's my opinion."

"How do you propose to deal with those conflicts? Joaquín tells us he was making a real effort to stay clean. What guarantee can you give me that he won't run into trouble again?"

Mr. Baker's face pulled into a frown. "I have a little operation going on with some parolees living together in an old-fashioned boardinghouse, with a landlady acting as a mother-figure to them. I've talked to her, and to the other boys, and they'll accept Joaquín as a resident."

"I've heard of the home," the judge said. "In fact, one or two of your boys have been back through here."

"We lose a boy now and then," Mr. Baker admitted. "But in general I think the balance is more towards success than failure. It's a place where a boy makes good or strikes out with no one else to blame. He has the same access to drugs and other kinds of trouble that he'd have living at home. He can work, go to school, or ditch. But if he messes up, the law's out there waiting for him. What the home offers is the support and example of other boys who are making it—as well as of a few who aren't. All we can offer any offender is a chance to make his own decision. And the home, I feel, does that."

Judge Closson looked at Keeny's mother.

"Mrs. Durán, do you have any feelings about your son being placed in the home?"

Keeny's mother let her hands fly up in a gesture of despair. "It would be just like the Aztecs! You can't put out a fire with more fire. He should go to work.

We need the money and it would keep him out of trouble."

"I'll go to work part-time," Keeny said.

Mrs. Durán held Armando close. "We'd never see the money, Your Honor."

"In any event, you'd see it or you wouldn't, wherever the boy was living," said the judge. He laid his hands on Keeny's file and his lower lip pulled across the upper. After a moment he said:

"I'm going to rule in favor of placing the boy in the parolee house."

Chapter 27

Keeny carried a large paper bag, nearly empty, up the outside stairway of the parolee house. The stairway, a sort of airy scaffolding, had the flimsy construction of a roller coaster, a dizzy, hung-from-a-star feeling, with glimpses of the ground thirty feet below. The house seemed to have been built without inside stairways, or perhaps it had been a single-story dwelling to begin with, and, as stories were added, like layers to a cake, stairways had had to be nailed to the back wall for access.

The boy named Shelly was leading the way. A view of the night-lighted city developed as they climbed, dark hills clustered with lights, red taillights trickling like rubies along the busier streets. Over all hung a mist stained with the glow of the city.

They reached a landing and went into a long, dim room whose ceiling was the V-shaped roof of the house. The only light in the room came from an illuminated beer-sign set in one wall. There were four beds in the room, mere mattresses and box springs placed on the floor. On two of them boys were dozing as they waited for dinner. One of them was Andy; the other was the loner called Manny.

"Your bed's the one in the far corner," Shelly said. "How do you like the pad?" He looked around with pride.

"Great," Keeny said. A couple of psychedelic candles flashed on and off like Christmas tree lights. Incense was burning and a radio played softly in the shadows. Posters were tacked to the rafters overhead. There was even a small desk, in case someone wanted to study.

Keeny put his suitcase on the corner bed and sat down. A good feeling was coming. Shelly stood looking at him.

"What do you turn on to?" he asked.

Keeny shrugged. "You name it. But I'm putting everything down, now. I haven't dropped anything for over a week."

Manny turned a disgusted glance in his direction. "If there's anything I don't dig, it's a hypocrite!" he mocked. "Don't be giving me no lectures about being a good citizen, man—just because you've been off pills for a week."

"Well, I'm *trying* to put them down," Keeny amended. "I don't really care what anybody else does," he added, "so don't worry about the lectures."

"I'm just telling you," repeated Manny.

Keeny's temper gave a tug. But, on reflection, he realized that Manny was probably loaded, and that was why he was abusive. He looked for a place to unpack.

"Where do you put your stuff?" he asked.

Shelly said, "Leave it in the bag tonight. Peggy will give you a foot-locker to put behind the bed. But keep your money on you. I got burned for twelve dollars and a cigarette lighter before I learned that."

Manny sat up. "Are you accusing me?" he said belligerently.

Shelly yawned. "No, no, man. I'm just saying you've done time for burglary, and you might break into somebody's drawer by instinct before you knew you were burning a friend."

Keeny grinned. From his bed, Andy said with a yawn, "Hey, what time is it?"

"Time to go downstairs before the hogs get all the food," Shelly said.

The boys crowded onto the outside landing and thundered down the frail stairway. Keeny, at the end of the line, asked Andy: "What's Peggy like?"

"Like? There's nobody like Peggy, man. She's like a cop, or somebody's mother, or your favorite warden."

Manny called back: "She's inconsistent. Some days you can show up full of reds and she won't say a thing. And then, like last night, she busts me for a can of beer! I'm getting out of here. I can't hack it."

"When?" asked Andy.

"When I pay her what I owe her. I'm in to her for eighty dollars back board."

They reached a porch behind the kitchen. Inside, Keeny could see a big man in a cook's cap working at a huge restaurant stove. He saw Mrs. Sherwood carrying a tray into the dining room. Andy opened the door and went through the kitchen to the dining room. Through the open door there came to Keeny a delicious aroma of pork chops and coffee. In the fragrance there was something deep and moving, something beyond food. It was a promise, a hope, a chance, the only chance he was asking—to strike out or to make good, with no one to blame and no one to slow him down.

Mrs. Sherwood saw him in the doorway, and smiled and said, "Better hurry up, Keeny. You don't know these guys."

Keeny grinned, hitched up his pants, and hurried in to start the new life of Keeny Durán.